STRAY DOG

Richard John Parfitt

THIRD MAN BOOKS

Copyright ©2023 by Richard J. Parfitt

Third Man Books, LLC
623 7th Ave S
Nashville, TN 37203

A CIP record is on file with the Library of Congress.

Cover and book design by Amin Qutteineh.

Printed in the Czech Republic.

ISBN: 979-8-98661-451-9

Preface to Stray Dogs. xi

Part One - Toronto
Incident on Yonge Street. 3
The Collegiate Institute 9
Frankie Lee. 13
Niagara Falls. 19
Randy Miller. 25
Exhibition Place 31
The Douchebag of Toronto. 35
Romeo Silva 39
The Neon D 45

Part Two - Into This World We're Thrown
The Summerhouse 55
Lake of Fire. 59
The Spirit Board. 65
Janice Morningstar. 69
The Hut in the Woods 73
The Booksellers. 79
The Devil's Children 85
The White River Motelier 93
The Names 99
Welcome Stranger. 107

Part Three - Toronto
At the Treatment Centre 115
Frankie Lee. 119
Exhibition Place 123
Romeo Silva 129
The Neon D 135
The Summerhouse 139
Stray Dogs. 143
The Collegiate Institute 147
Mount Hope Cemetery 153

Biography. 157
Acknowledgments 159
Note on some sources 161

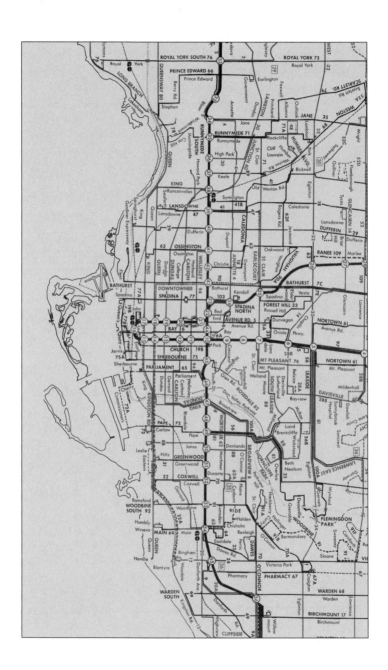

Outside the city are the dogs—the sorcerers, the sexually immoral, the murderers, the idol worshipers, and all who love to live a lie.

– Revelation 22:15

To the memory of Robert White

PREFACE TO STRAY DOGS

Stray Dogs is set in Toronto at the end of the 1970s.

In those days, downtown was notorious for its Sin Strip, comprising four blocks on Yonge, between Gerrard and Dundas. They were loaded with strip joints, adult bookstores, rub 'n tugs and movie theatres which, according to *The Globe and Mail*, made it one of the 'largest concentrations of sex-related businesses in North America'. It was a place of tension and, sometimes, menace. The Halloween parade of drag queens and costumed revellers would draw thousands of fascinated spectators as well as a heavy-handed mob of 'suburban punks' ready to pelt them with eggs.

Peter Porter wrote, 'No single imagination can truly own a city,' and that 'we are really clearing a space in our minds where specific happenings and feelings may be identified and reconvened.'

Stray Dogs is an evocation of a half-remembered city. The story and its characters are fictional. Any relation to people living, or dead, is entirely coincidental.

RJP

PART ONE

Toronto

INCIDENT ON YONGE STREET

If there was something Dickensian about our circumstance, then Romeo was Fagin. He was also a fat slob and looked like a sack of shit with a piece of string tied around the middle. He was a mean bastard as well. Romeo Silva's idea of fun was to buy two dozen eggs and drive around the city egging queers and old people. His business was black market sales and he sold anything he could get his hands on: lightbulbs, kitchen knives, microwaves, juice blenders, rare and unusual antiques, girly mags and blue films.

With us it was dictionaries.

Romeo would keep the car running while a bunch of high school dropouts hit the office blocks and industrial estates cold selling to the typists. The Merriam-Webster books were available at a

3

limited supply and for a discounted price of $20.00 [including luxury box]. For each copy sold we made $4.00.

The leather-bound dictionaries were remaindered rejects on account of the page numbers being all mixed up and in the wrong order.

You had to know how to turn the pages so as not to arouse suspicion.

You had to work fast and make your pitch before security threw you out. The crew was made up of a runt with a lazy eye, and a dirty blonde in a red sweater and jeans. And then there was me:

William Turner. A long way from home.

Ray had gotten a job selling tents and camping supplies for a big outlet in Toronto. 'This is it, Turner,' he'd say. 'A new life, a fresh start.'

Moving in with the old man had seemed like a good idea at the time, but now I wasn't so sure. School wasn't working out and I'd started hanging at the park fixing hot knives through a cardboard toilet roll with the stoners.

'People make mistakes,' Ray said.

I thought he was talking about me but he was talking about my mother.

'She'll be back. Just you wait and see. All this foolishness will work itself out.'

I wasn't so sure about that. My mother had been gone six months already and there was still no sign of her coming back. Sometimes I wished she were dead so we could at least make a big fuss about it. Could have remembered her as if she were Joan of Arc instead of the two words Ray used when she left.

*

It was late September and we'd been cruising around looking for targets when we spotted the golden arches rising up against the bright blue of a big sky. None of us had eaten breakfast, so we stopped for something to eat. Romeo juggled some eggs while Millboy went inside to collect the order. When Millboy got back we stuffed ourselves with burgers and shakes – stinking the car up with cheese pickle and sugar syrup. When we were done, Romeo spotted an old man crossing a gas station forecourt and nailed him with a direct hit. What he didn't see were the two boys coming out the store wondering why their father was wiping raw egg off his bald head.

Romeo spat out his Big Mac and turned and burned onto Yonge while a black Corvette pulled off and started to tail us – the faces inside a fixed expression of ferocious intent and foreseeable violence. They were older, bigger, and a bunch of street rats had just humiliated their old man.

We raced through the streets, weaving in and out of traffic and running a red light before turning into a side street and coming to a dead end where we reversed a U-turn, just as the Corvette pulled in and blocked our exit. The two boys got out the car and started walking towards us gripping tyre irons.

Some kids playing at stamping on ants stopped to watch the show.

We hunkered down on the backseat while Romeo gunned the engine. As the boys got closer you could see their faces cratered with zits. One of em raised a tyre iron and a handful of sparks burst in the sunshine as we smashed into the side of the black Corvette, almost taking the door off. The tyre iron bounced off the roof of Romeo's Buick and clanged on the road behind. Millboy pushed up against the back window and gave em the finger.

The chase was back on.

*

We zigzagged and played the traffic for a while but couldn't shake em off. We went up on the Expressway and lost em in the rush but took a curve too fast and hit the central reservation. The Buick went up on its side, slip sliding across the freeway before smashing into a pile of blown out tyres and then slamming back down and coming to rest diagonal to the oncoming traffic.

In the screaming chaos of slow-motion terror, me and Frankie banged heads and hit the backrests hard. Millboy cannonballed through the middle and smashed his face on the console. Blood was pouring out of his busted nose and he sat dazed, trying to stem the bleeding with a shaky hand. During the crashing, two dozen eggs had taken off and splattered us all in a yolky mess. Flecks of shell and yellow snot decorated the inside of the car and seemed to offset the seriousness of the occasion.

Within seconds of coming to a halt, Romeo had freed himself and was now running up the embankment and heading for the cover of the trees. The black Corvette cruised up slow, took one look at us and then sped off.

Karmic payback.

The cops must have wondered what three teenage misfits covered in egg sitting amongst the detritus of the world's finest dictionaries could possibly have been doing. They took us to Mount Sinai where they checked our heads and X-rayed our bones and called our parents, or the ones we had.

When Ray showed up he was overwhelmed with trying to understand what had happened. 'I thought you were in school?' he said. 'You've dragged me out of work. What's the matter with you? Christ Almighty, Turner.'

Frankie's mother looked straight at me and then at Millboy who was grinning on account of all the medication he'd taken.

'What is it, Frances,' she said. 'Is it drugs? Is it one of these boys?'

Randy Miller had a great wad of cotton wool taped across the middle of his face. The cops had to stop his grandfather from battering him even more. Instead, Gramps Miller settled for yelling at Millboy, at least until he got him back to the safety of his own home. The cops wanted to know about Romeo. They wanted to know about the dictionaries and the car.

What was it with the eggs.

THE COLLEGIATE INSTITUTE

Back in school the other kids kept their distance. I'd sit in the canteen and eat alone. Walk home alone. Mr. Carpenter was the one teacher I felt a connection with, but I'd messed up the first week when he asked my name and I said John Turner instead of my real name which is William Turner. I have no idea why I did this. Maybe it was because I never felt comfortable with the name William and thought starting again in a new place meant I could reinvent myself as John. My cover got blown when we were looking at a poem about somebody lost in the woods.

I shall be telling this with a sigh
Somewhere ages and ages hence:

Two roads diverged in a wood

I knew this poem because Ray had it on a fridge magnet back at the apartment. It has something to do with the choices we make and where they lead us. Mr. Carpenter said it was a triumph of self-assertion, and a celebration of something called individualism, but I wasn't so sure. Seems to me the poet is just making himself feel better about a decision he made. Like Ray making a new life for himself and forgetting that I didn't have any choice in the matter. I put my hand up to make this point. Mr. Carpenter was thrilled that someone would actually ask a question and called out to me excitedly as John. The class went silent, expecting him to realise his mistake.

No mistake.

The class exploded into a riot of laughter. The fake kind when someone's laughing so hard it's just an expression of cruelty. I laughed with them so they thought I'd set old Carpenter up rather than reveal the strangeness of what I'd done.

Mr. Carpenter took the whole thing personally and sent me to the principal's office where I got a warning: 'We had high hopes for you, Turner. But you've let us all down. You've let your father down and you've let Mr. Carpenter down, but most of all, you've let yourself down. I can smell pot? Have you been smoking in the yard? Are you far out man?'

It was just another reason to stop going to school.

When they called home to find out why I wasn't attending, Ray grabbed me by the shirt and held me up against the wall and called me a bastard. I thought he was going to hit me, but then all the life went out of him, and he turned and walked away.

'I don't know what to do with you,' he said.

I didn't care much.

Ray didn't get back from work till late most nights so I'd grab a TV dinner from the freezer – an aluminium tray with compartments containing peas and potatoes and some tough meaty stuff in gravy. In the top right corner was an apple crumble which I ate first.

I spent my time watching the Gong Show or jerking off into a sock. When Ray got home we drifted around the apartment like ghosts. Sometimes I'd meet him in the hallway or hear him on the telephone talking to someone I thought might be my mother, and I'd rush in, but he'd wave me away and close the door and I'd go back to my room and lay on my bed reading or just listening to music.

*

I dreamed about her a lot. Kept pictures in a notebook. Photographs stolen from the family album. A child wearing a cheap summer dress surrounded by her sisters. Bony knees and a big smile. Then, as a teenager, cramped into a passport photo booth – wide eyed and wearing her hair up like a movie star. Colour snaps with Ray on a daytrip to the seaside.

He's holding onto her, but she's pulling away. Even then.

My mother sent me postcards. They seem to come from all over. New York. Quebec. Unless I got to the mailbox first, my father took them.

He said we didn't need to hear from her.

Some got through. One of the Horseshoe Falls – the way the fierce white rush of the water fell into that serene lake. The cars lining up like bright toys along the big river: "From Goat Island to Rainbow Bridge"

Just so you know where I am X

She sent me books too. One was a mad story about a boy who wakes up to find himself trapped in the body of a giant bug. The boy starts panicking because he can't leave the room and his father is hammering on the door.

I wondered why he didn't just open the window and fly away.

FRANKIE LEE

Frankie Lee lived with her mother in Regent Park. The housing sat squat in the shadow of the big city towers. The pathway that led to the apartments reminded me of a maze designed to keep you from escaping. From the gloomy shadows of Regent Park, you could see downtown lit up like a thousand Christmas trees. The apartment had the least amount of furniture of any I'd ever seen. No books, not even a record player. Magazines were piled up on the Chesterfield while cosmetics were spread out over a coffee table. Some picture cards. Lotions. Potions. Trinkets hanging from the doorframe. Crystal stones. Feathers. Good luck charms and scented candles.

Frankie convinced me that I needed to pierce my ear. It had to be the left one, otherwise people might get the wrong idea. She took two cubes of ice from the freezer and held the bottom portion of my ear in an ice vice until it went numb, then started stabbing at it with a safety pin until it looked like a meatball.

Blood streamed down my neck and over my shirt collar so she taped a giant twist of cotton wool to the side of my head so I looked like Van Gogh in that picture where he's wearing the blue hunting cap.

'Maybe I need something sharper?' she said.

'Oh, it's nothing,' I said, my head on fuckin fire and half my ear destroyed.

It had been three weeks since the crash so we took a streetcar downtown – the cotton wool on my ear wet with blood and Millboy hanging upside down from the handrail making sounds like an ape with his nose all taped up. When people stared I stared back until they looked away.

We got off at Yonge and Dundas and walked past the adult bookstores and strip clubs. Voices from the doorways calling out to Frankie.

'Hey Blondie, wanna make a film?'

We walked past the Chinese Food Man next to the Rio. Old guys playing chess on the street and smoking cigars. Greased hair and pot bellies. Past the Angels' clubhouse. Bikes all polished chrome with death head skulls painted on the tanks. The Angels stood around laughing wildly and drinking from bottles – their shaved heads glowing like plasma balls under the neon beer signs. A few mean looking girls dressed in capped sleeve tee shirts and denim shorts threw us dirty looks.

We gave em a wide berth and kept on walking.

We walked into the hinterland of an industrial sprawl where vagrants, curb crawlers, and the red eyes of night creatures flashed like hot coals in the darkness.

Soon the sound of the streets quieted. As we strolled up on to the Expressway, the headlights blurred as the shape of the city rose like a cut-out in the distance. The tall tower like some great hypodermic needle reflected in the black mirror of the lake.

We searched along the roadside kicking through the shrub. Our faces small and pale in the darkness. We spooked at every sound. The sudden rush of traffic or beat of a batwing. The scream of a fox. We walked for what seemed like an hour but may have just been ten minutes and came to a stretch that looked familiar. Millboy was swatting at bugs and getting fed up.

'I'm getting fed up,' he said.

Frankie said, 'Try and remember, will you?'

Millboy sat on the ground and pulled a joint from his pocket. It fell apart so he glued it back together with spit. The flare of the match lit up his broken face like a Halloween mask and sparks popped like miniature fireworks burning tiny craters in his jeans. 'You heard that howling earlier,' he said. 'A coyote can smell blood from miles away.'

'There's no coyotes round here,' Frankie said.

'Hitchhiker got ripped up by one last month.'

'That's a lie,' Frankie said.

'He came across one eating a dead moose. Turned him into dog food.'

'That's a lie,' Frankie said again.

Millboy started coughing – like he might lose a lung. His whole body shaking from the strength of a harsh toke. He took another hit and held it in and croaked.

'There's not a lot of meat on you, but they like em bony.'

In the quiet of the night, you could hear the buzz of your own blood rush through your veins. The insects moving in the long grass. As our eyes adjusted to the darkness our vision sharpened and the highway took on a perspective that somehow seemed familiar.

'This looks right,' Millboy said. 'Just over there.'

Over there was a broad scrape across the blacktop, upon which scattered pieces of glass like some warped image of the night sky. Up ahead and to the side was a pile of scrap tyres. I walked over and reached my hand into the rim of one before pulling out the canvas bag of money as if it were a rabbit from a hat.

'Is this what you're looking for?'

'Peachy creamo,' Millboy said.

'Hey, Turner,' Frankie said. 'You got the magic touch.'

*

In a restroom cubicle downtown, we counted out over a thousand bucks. Millboy bought some speed from a street vendor and we snorted a line through a drinking straw in a McDonald's and played pinball in Funland before ending up late night at a Baskin Robbins, famous for its supreme ice cream.

The three of us sat at the Formica table all clown smiles from the raspberry and chocolate smears around our chops. Under the fluorescent tubing Frankie's hair lit up like a halo. When she leaned back her sweater rode up revealing her belly and some pubic hair that poked out the top of her jeans.

'We're just taking our cut, right?' she said. 'Romeo owes us on those sales, but we're just keeping the money safe for him?'

'We're just keeping it safe,' I said. 'Anyway, he'll think the cops took it so it doesn't matter.'

'It doesn't matter,' Millboy said. 'The cops took it.'

NIAGARA FALLS

We lived under a flightpath. In a townhouse – a multi-unit complex with shared parking and a laundry room featuring a main corridor that ran through the entire building. From my bedroom window, I could see the flyover heading toward the Plaza or back into town. No birds sang. Just a constant stream of traffic and the roar from the planes overhead. From a shoebox under the bed I took the postcard and went into the kitchen where Ray was burning the toast.

'What is that?' he said, opening the window.

'It's from Frankie,' I lied.

'The girl from the car accident and the boy with the crazy eye? The ones I saw at Mount Sinai with that old drunk and that woman? And by the way, I know what she does for a living.'

'How do you know what she does for a living?'

'Don't get smart with me.'

Ray scraped the burned bits off the toast with a butter knife. The black crumbs were going all over the place. His shoelace was undone and he was trying to knot his tie at the same time and getting grease on his shirt collar. Eventually the toast broke in half and he tossed both slices in the sink.

'Stay away from those people, Turner. They're bad news.'

'They're my friends.'

'They're not your friends,' he said. 'I spoke to your school and they told me you'd fallen in with some bad company.'

'You spoke to Mr. Carpenter?'

'I did, and he's willing to give you a second chance.'

'What did he say?'

'That you're never there, and when you are, you're half asleep. Where the hell do you go all day?'

I wanted to tell Ray about the money. That Millboy wasn't bad at all. I wanted to tell him about Frankie.

'Can I ask you a question?' I said.

Ray put a five down on top of the television. 'Not now,' he said. 'I have to get to work. Get something to eat at the Mall or there's a TV dinner in the refrigerator.'

*

It was a two-hour ride from Union Station, so I found a seat and stared out of the window. Bright yellow fields. Walls and bridges. But the regular click-clacking of the track got me daydreaming and I must have dozed off because before I knew it we were pulling into Niagara Falls.

It was the end of the tourist season but there were still plenty of people around. Mostly families and old folk and some in wheelchairs, joking around under the spray that came up from the river. I walked over to the rails and stared down at the rush of white water. The churn of the whirlpool. You could see why people might jump in. Seemed like a good idea if you gazed long enough.

It was a sunny day and you could get your picture taken with a person dressed like Barney Rubble for a dollar. I sat in the flower garden eating a Mr. Submarine and reread the message again. The postcard was a freebee. The kind they give away in the reception area of hotels just to get some advertising.

The hotels were all lined up along the waterfront but this one had a great big green and yellow plastic billboard on top of the roof that said *Quality Inn*. I must have spent an hour getting up the nerve, but when I finally went over she was just sitting there on the terrace drinking a coffee like it had been no time at all.

'You'll have had the postcards then?' she said. 'I thought maybe your father had thrown them away.'

I had a lot of things I wanted to say but couldn't find the right words. She offered me a cigarette and we sat squinting in the bright sun and smoking.

'How's school?' she said.

'Not going so well.'

'It's not the end of the world.'

'Why'd you go?' I said.

'I can't remember.'

'Was it Ray?'

'It doesn't matter anymore.'

'Is this where you live now?' I said.

'It's where I live right now,' she said.

'There's a girl,' I said. 'I really like her.'

'What's her name?'

'Frankie.'

'That's a boy's name.'

'It's a girl's name too. It means Frances.'

'I'm just joking. Is she as pretty as me?'

My mother blew me a smoky kiss and laughed. The skin from a cold cup of coffee hung on her lip like a piece of tissue paper. Her green dress was close-fitting and her soft flesh spilled out, flushing red in the heat. When she leaned over, I could smell sour milk, the dirty earth, the sea.

She seemed smaller than I remembered. Small-boned like a bird. The lines under her eyes visible in a way I had not seen before. The powdery makeup on her face as fine as dust.

We walked along the shopfronts arm in arm and ended up watching a movie at the Seneca Theatre – some garbage with Dustin Hoffman. When we came out it was still daylight but getting breezy. The coloured illuminations hung like giant fairy lights above Niagara.

'Look at that,' I said.

'You can always see a rainbow over the Falls,' she said, 'it's nothing special.'

It looked special to me.

When we got back to the *Quality Inn* there was a man waiting. He was younger than her and dressed in a wide necked green shirt and flares. He flashed a nervous smile and had shiny hair. I wanted to punch him in the face.

'He's just a friend,' she said. 'Come back and see me, will you?'

When I got to the street corner I looked back to see if she was still there but she was gone.

Her friend was gone too.

RANDY MILLER

The days burned faster than I can remember. Roller skating at the Terrace. Hanging at the Eton, and when it got too hot, riding the subway just for kicks. The three of us went everywhere together: The Cherry Street Drive In, Sam the Record Man, the SkyDome. The money went fast. Frankie had her hair cut in a downtown salon – bleached short and a leather jacket too. There was a movie she wanted to see. She bought ice skates. I bought records and books and a new pair of jeans. Millboy bought a Zippo, a new pair of runners and one of them velvet blacklight posters of a huge breasted woman that he pinned to his bedroom wall and admired regularly. But mostly he just fed coins into the machines down on the Strip.

King, Queen, Dundas, College, Wellesley and Bloor.

Downtown was a playground. The grindhouse theatres were somewhere to get out of the rain and smoke a cigarette; low budget Kung Fu and porno. Buy one ticket and stay all day or maybe take a nap.

We slept in each other's beds or sometimes stayed out all night. Anywhere but home.

One night me and Millboy laid in bed and shared a puny joint, watching the toxic rings of smoke swirl around a red-light bulb as if it were some far out planet. Gramps came in and told us to turn the music down.

We considered the situation, then turned it up.

Millboy said, 'He's not even my real Gramps.'

'How do you mean?' I said.

'Miller is his name not mine. He married Nana after my real Gramps died.'

'Where's your Nana?'

'Dead too. We're a cursed family.'

'How do you mean?' I said again.

'I was born dead and came back to life. That's why I'm so small and got a crazy eye. They put me in some acid to finish me off, but instead of killing me, it jumpstarted my engine, and here I am today. If it wasn't for a kind-natured nurse I would have ended up in the garbage with the amputated parts of the less fortunate. My medical records clearly state the following, that I entered this world late term and unable to survive outside the womb. The only reason I'm still alive is the fact that the abortionist had not yet arrived to work that morning.'

'What about your mother?' I said.

'Died the day I was born.'

'You're a fighter.'

'One in three.'

'How do you mean?' I said it again

'I should have been twins, only my brother got stuck up there and killed em both dead. I'm the only one who made it out alive. They buried em out at Mount Hope.'

'Do you know who your father is?' I said.

'Elvis Presley,' Millboy said.

'That's a goddamn lie,' I said.

'It's not beyond the realms of possibility,' Millboy said. 'In 1963 my mother was working as a waitress at the Charlotte Motor Speedway in North Carolina. The King was making a movie at the same place, and took full advantage of the situation. It's a well-known fact that the King liked young girls, and my mother would have been a young girl at the time.'

'There were plenty of young girls available to the King,' I said. 'He could have had the pick of anyone.'

'My mother was always the most beautiful,' Millboy said. 'And twins run in the family.'

'What family?' I said.

'On my father's side,' he said.

He kept rattling on but I must've fallen asleep.

When I woke up, Millboy was wrapped around me like a limpet. Sticky and his breath like an open grave. Gramps Miller was flat out on the recliner with his trousers around his ankles sweating out the booze. We went through his pockets and took what he had before heading over to Regent Park where Kathy Lee was smoking furiously and boiling an egg.

Mrs. Lee was wearing a pair of red, white, and blue ski boots, and a see-through nightie with a gold lame bikini underneath – looking like Wonder Woman, except for the smoking and the egg. Millboy said she was a belly dancer and you could see her shake it for five bucks down at a titty bar on Wednesday afternoons.

Kathy Lee stared straight at Millboy and then rubbed the corner of her eye with the tip of her index finger and pulled the skin back so that the red rim turned inside out to give her the look of a lizard.

'You're not normal,' she said.

When Frankie came in, she picked up her mother's cigarettes and lit one up. Kathy Lee dropped her own cigarette into the scalding water and spooned the egg out of the pan, juggling it to the drainer, where it sat, steaming and cracked.

'You're too young for smoking,' she said.

'Same age you were when you had me,' Frankie said.

'What about your egg?' Kathy Lee said, but we were halfway out the door.

*

We crossed Dundas and headed south, Frankie took my hand and pressed it against her bony ribs and I could feel her heart racing away. The push and drag of her breathing. The sweet curve under the sweater. I was lovesick but not inexperienced. I'd already popped my cherry in the communal laundry room with the girl from next door.

Frankie said, 'I think I'm having a heart attack.'

I kept my hand there. 'You're all right,' I said. 'Let's get something to eat.'

We walked down to the harbourfront and ate breakfast at Captain John's: French toast with butter and syrup, and then shared what was left of the money. Millboy had two breakfasts.

'How come you're so skinny?' I said.

'I need to eat twice as much as a normal person.'

'How come?'

'Heartworm,' he said. 'It's a disease where a bunch of maggots take up residence in your ventricles rent free. Slows you down and poisons your blood. It's a slow death but I reckon I got a few years yet. Dogs get it from licking each other's assholes.'

'Whose asshole you been licking?'

'You can get it from eating bugs or bad food.'

'You don't eat bugs.'

'Bugs in bad food. Sometimes they crawl into the sauce. I think that might be what happened.'

'That stuff you buy off the street?'

'It's not beyond the realms of possibility,' he was fond of saying.

Frankie sucked the goo from her fingers. 'Someone's calling me up all the time,' she said. 'They're saying dirty things.'

'What kind of dirty things?' I said.

'Like they want to bang me. Bone me. When I ask who it is they don't answer. When Kathy Lee answers they put the phone down. It's like they know who I am but I don't know who they are. I think it's Romeo. He could be the Douchebag, right?'

At this time, The Douchebag of Toronto was making a name for himself by going up to girls and saying: Do you know who The Douchebag of Toronto is? Then he'd show them his wang. If that didn't answer the question he took a knife out. The reports were that he was of heavy build with long greasy hair. He wore a flasher's mac. I heard he had a potato nose. Someone said his eyeballs were black. A cat had been found crucified, nailed to a door by its paws. Its screaming so distressing that the local college were offering counselling to any students affected. It was said that the Douchebag would break into apartments and dress up in girls' clothes and jerk off leaving a spunky glaze over the college textbooks as a reminder of who was in charge.

He was nicknamed the fat masturbator. The cat killer.

Students were advised to travel in pairs and carry whistles.

'Romeo's not the Douchebag,' I said.

'Well he could be,' Frankie said. 'Anyway, he knows we took the money.'

'How does he know?' I said.

'Tell him, Millboy.'

'Romeo saw me in the arcades when I was feeding the slots and followed me into the washroom. He pushed his fat gut up against me and said we took him for three thousand bucks. I said it was only a thousand.'

'Oh Jesus,' I said. 'What does he want?'

'His money back.'

EXHIBITION PLACE

We took the bus to Lakeshore and elbowed our way through the crowd. Everywhere people queued. They queued for the Ghost Train, the Yo-Yo, the Kamikaze and Hurricane Jets. The smell of candy apples and diesel fumes carried on the breeze and made us woozy with expectation. There were sideshows and street performers and someone called Elastic Man outside a marquee, pulling his arm skin-tight like a batwing and pressing a torch to the membrane so that it looked like he was lit up from the inside.

'Come on in,' he said. 'Freaks and Fat Ladies. Natural Wonders of the World.'

Inside were sad looking farm animals with growths on their backs and midgets dressed in medieval clothes, while shoved over in the corner of the tent was a great big fat lady eating a cake. Marzipan sugar fell like soft flakes of snow and powdered on her lap. Above her head, a sign:

Guess my Weight.

Millboy said, 'I'm one hundred pounds and I reckon you're seven of me.'

The great big fat lady put down the cake and wiped her mouth with a chubby mitt before standing up with the help of two sticks. You could smell the stink coming off her like unwashed clothes or a dog breathing right in your face. She walked over to a glass cabinet full of plastic toys and hard candy, her chest clattering like a rattlesnake.

'Choose carefully,' she said.

Millboy pointed at a shiny, black water pistol.

'I'll take the gun,' he said.

When we got to the Gooderham Fountain, Romeo was waiting. It was hotter than hell and he was stuffing himself with chicken wings. The grease ran down his chin and spotted his shirt, which was soaked with sweat rings anyhow. His gut hung over his jeans like a 4-litre bag of fresh milk and his zipper was undone and a piece of shirt poked out like a tiny dick, as he spoke with his mouth full.

'The teen dream,' he said. 'Where've you been?'

The way Romeo stared at Frankie made my stomach churn, and I hawked up some phlegm and spat on the floor.

Millboy had removed the dressing from his face, revealing two yellowing black eyes and a giant scab on the bridge of his nose. 'We had to go to the hospital,' he said. 'My nose was all busted up.'

'You're all right now, aren't you?' Romeo said. 'Look better if you ask me.'

Romeo pointed to the side of my head and said, 'Nice earing, Turner.'

'Want do you want,' I said.

'I got a job for you. Do it and I'll write off the money you owe me.'

'And if we don't?' Millboy said.

Romeo crumpled the greaseproof paper into a ball and bounced it off Millboy's skull. 'I'll write you off,' he said.

Romeo Silva walked off in the direction of the Princes' Gates as Millboy filled the pistol from the fountain and took aim. I could see Frankie fixed on a thought like she was trying to figure out whether Romeo was the one making the phone calls.

'Romeo's not the Douchebag,' I said.

We watched the Dog Swim before stuffing ourselves with popcorn and then lay on the grassy bank trying to work out what a thousand-dollar job might be.

'Maybe he wants his house painted?' Millboy said. 'Or a blowjob?'

'The thousand-dollar suck off,' Frankie said. 'You boys got your work cut out.'

She jerked the pistol into her mouth and spat out.

'Anyway, I think he's got the hots for Randy.'

'Maybe he wants someone killed?' Millboy said. 'That'll cost about a thousand bucks?'

'Then why don't you kill him?' Frankie said. 'That's a thousand-dollar problem solved right there.'

Frankie closed one eye like on television and fired the pistol.

Millboy wiped the spray from his face. 'Maybe I will,' he said.

'Attaboy,' Frankie said.

Millboy went off to the rifle range to get some practice in while me and Frankie took to the cover of the trees where she stretched back in the long grass and I pushed my hand down the front of her pants. After I finished she wiped the mess off her jeans with some big leaves and we walked back to the rides where I'd promised to take her on the Ferris Wheel.

THE DOUCHEBAG OF TORONTO

It had been raining and the air was cool and fresh. Black pools of water shone in the neon that now illuminated the shop fronts of Queen Street. We'd spent what was left of the money and had been to see the *Invasion of the Body Snatchers* and then on to a steak house. As we got close to the corner of Moss Park, the wind picked up and shook the leaves and somebody stepped out wearing a long grey coat. As we got closer I could smell his fusty breath and damp clothes. His skin was sallow and cratered with acne scars. His beard and hair a greasy mop even by street standards. We tried to keep walking but he positioned himself in such a way that we couldn't pass. Frankie's hand gripped tight in mine. Her palm clammy. The man in the long grey coat staring straight at us – his eyes small and black like a scorpion.

He said, 'You kids got a light?'

Frankie took out her lighter and he gripped her shaky fist, taking a long deep drag before pushing her hand away and exhaling up into the twilight. Night bugs dancing in his smoky breath. 'You know who I am?' he said. 'I'm The Douchebag of Toronto. I'm the Douchebag and I've got a knife.'

He patted the breast pocket on his raincoat so as to indicate where he kept it. I laughed nervously and pulled at Frankie's arm, stepping out onto the street and walking around him, but he kept following while shouting all the time.

'I'm the Douchebag. The Douchebag of Toronto. You heard of me?'

I told Frankie to run and she ran with me running right behind to make sure she was okay. I kept expecting the Douchebag to grab my collar or stick me with a blade. Meanwhile his voice like a sonic boom echoing through the streets downtown.

'Hey! You know who I am?'

When we got to Regent Park, Frankie was too scared to tell her mother, so instead we sat at the kitchen table taking forever to finish our coffee and saying it looked like heavy rain and waiting for Kathy Lee to go to bed so I could crash on the Chesterfield. But Kathy Lee was giving us a stone-cold look that said 'no way,' and fumbled around in the closet and found me an old coat.

*

A thread of gold had weaved itself through the night sky and brightened the bleak streets downtown. At one point I thought I saw the

Douchebag but it turned out to be a drunk woman in a long coat holding one high heel shoe while looking for the other. She stared for a moment, trying to work out who I was before realising I was a nobody, and then pulled up her dress and squatted down to take a leak in the gutter before falling into some boxes and yelling at me.

'I don't care who you are. I will eat you alive.'

I stayed off the main drag and took the alleyways. Some dogs were scavenging through garbage. I kicked the metal roller doors and they loped off into the night. I knew I'd missed the last train back but at least it was warm, and as the drizzle seeped through the waxy coat and onto my skin, I bent down in a doorway to make myself as small as possible and watched the sun rise over the city before making my way back home.

The traders were setting up their stalls and leaving the boxes on the sidewalk as they unloaded the trucks. I stole some oranges from a crate and kept walking. The sounds of the street growing with the early traffic. The morning drizzle mixed with the fog. Barrels of crabmeat and trays of fat silver fish salt scented the air and made the pavement sloppy with melting ice.

The city coming to life. The muted rumble becoming a roar.

The subway home jolted and jerked and kept me awake. When I got back Ray was just leaving for work. He shook his head as we passed in the doorway.

'Who the hell do you think you are?' He said.

There was a half-eaten packet of Hostess Chips on the kitchen table. I crammed what was left in my mouth and sliced open the oranges and sucked the sugar from the fruit before going up to my room wondering if we'd really met the Douchebag or just some creep who liked scaring kids.

ROMEO SILVA

Coloured lights were strung across Yonge and people came up from the subways and packed onto trams clutching bags and gifts. Street vendors were selling hot cashew nuts and the smell of greasy meat hung in the air, mixing with the spiced cider from the open markets. Young people gathered at the entrance to the Horseshoe or sat on the kerbstone holding their heads while inside some punk band were playing fast and loud. Miller was harassing by-passers for cigarettes when Frankie turned up with a fleabag kitten she'd picked up off the street.

'Lost cat,' she said, 'found it wandering, didn't I.'

The cat was a stripy ball of fur. It looked out from the top of Frankie's shirt and gave a pitiful little cough, before tucking its head back down. Frankie hadn't exactly found it wandering. It was in a box outside the animal shelter, but she knew what would happen if she didn't take it home.

'What's its name?' I said.

'Tiger. I'm going to bring her with us for good luck.'

'Watch out for the Douchebag,' I said.

Frankie made an angry face and wrapped her leather jacket tight around the kitten, just as an off-white Ford Maverick slowed and pulled up.

A car sticker on the rear fender:

Jesus Loves You, Everyone Else Thinks You're an Asshole.

Romeo Silva hauled himself out of the car and beckoned us into an entrance. We followed him up to the top of the stairwell where he unlocked a door and led us into a room full of junk. Boxes of video tapes and piles of books and a clothes' rail hung with tagged shirts—and on the floor, a tray of digital watches, and some cameras, too. He told us to wait and went back out, so I picked up a Polaroid Camera while Frankie struck a pose and I took a picture.

'Look at all this stuff,' I said. 'And he pays us four dollars for every twenty we make.'

The camera flashed and whirred and when the negative came out, Frankie took her nail and signed it with an X. 'Romeo don't care,' she said. 'He's just using us like he uses everyone else.'

Millboy was trying to feed the cat a stale donut. 'Romeo gave us a job when no one else would,' he said. 'Who else is going to give us work? We're not even old enough to finish school. And how about that time he gave me somewhere to stay when Gramps kicked me out? I would have been sleeping on the stairwells down-town if it wasn't for Romeo.'

Sometimes Millboy would take refuge in the towers. Hiding in the secret spaces that existed between the floors. He was like one of them roof rats. If Gramps beat him or he just got blue, he could disappear for weeks at a time. But, Millboy defending Romeo made me angry, and I said as much.

'Romeo used you as a lookout when his lockup was bust. Don't forget he left you on the Expressway covered in eggs and blood.'

'We threw them eggs too,' Millboy said. 'I seem to remember you asking me for a job.'

Millboy's words stung because they were true. Selling dictionaries was making me around ten dollars a day and it was the only job I could get. Romeo had a network of scams, and we were just another one of his crews. Outside the thrum of the traffic rattled the windows. The light from the city bled into the condensation and ran down the glass in coloured beads.

*

When Romeo came back into the room, he pulled up a crate and sat down and held out the keys to the Maverick. 'You just need pick up a small package and drop it off at Sault Ste. Marie,' he said. 'It's a special order and a simple job. Someone called Quohog will be waiting for you at the Neon D.'

'How will we recognise him?' Millboy said.

'He's got his name written on the back of his jacket.'

'What if he's not wearing his jacket?' Millboy said.

'He's got it written on his face too,' Romeo said. 'If you don't like it, find me a thousand dollars or work it out with the Devil's Children.'

41

East Toronto Angels. The ones we'd seen the night we took the money. The Children were a breakaway biker gang gone rogue. They cruised Union Station and the bus terminal looking for strays. They'd start by giving you a few dollars to work whatever con they were operating, then make you pay it off one way or another. They traded runaway girls for cigarettes. They trafficked stolen goods. It made sense Romeo was fencing for them. You stayed out of their way unless you wanted to get stomped.

'Sault Ste. Marie?' Millboy said. 'That's a thousand-mile trip.'

'No, it aint,' Romeo said. 'Anyway, you owe me a thousand fuckin bucks, asshole. That's one dollar a mile.'

'Yeah, but it's a thousand there and a thousand back,' Millboy said. 'That's two thousand miles and that means you owe us a thousand dollars.'

Millboy was the most simpleminded person I ever met. Calmly emanating wisdom while at the same time unable to hold a sensible thought in his head.

'What about some money?' I said. 'How're we gonna pay for gas and food?'

Romeo waved his hand at a large pile of dictionaries. 'Take some of those books,' he said. 'You know how to sell em, don't you?'

We took as many dictionaries as we could carry and went down onto the street where a small crowd of demonstrators waving *Pornography Must Go* signs stood around banging tambourines and singing.

Their voices in unison. Faces warped in prayer.

*

The Maverick had cracked vinyl seats and a silver radio dial. The hubcaps were missing and there was over 100,000 miles on the clock. I checked that the heater was working and that there was a spare and a toolkit but I wasn't sure if it would get us to our destination. Millboy thought the same and said as much.

'That car's a rotten bag of crap,' he said, 'and riddled with tin-worm.'

Romeo said, 'Just pick up the package from Quohog, deliver it, come back and dump the car downtown and then we'll be straight.'

'Even stevens,' I said.

'Damn straight,' Millboy said. 'Steven evens.'

We gassed up at the Circle K and drove out of the city and through the towns as the radio popped and fizzed and tuned itself to FM–playing the hits:

Stevie Nicks sang 'Dreams'.

By the time we reached the highway the sky was a patchwork of dark hues and silver shot through with a curious gold. After an hour we switched drivers and I jumped in the back and fingered Frankie under a coat and fell asleep and dreamed about my mother and awoke with a hard on feeling like a howling wind was blowing through my life.

THE NEON D

The waitress's hair hung down like a busted crow's wing and she wore a nametag that said Janice Morningstar. Over in the corner sat Quohog. There were solar suns and crescent moons randomly dotted on his skull and his arms were almost black from snake tattoos. When he saw Frankie, he rubbed his crotch and said, 'I can see you looking at my tattoos. I got a hundred and thirty-three of em. Even my balls got pictures on em. Had to shave my nut sack for that one. I'll show you if you want?'

'No thanks mister,' she said.

Quohog began to flick lit matches at Frankie. When she bent over to feed the cat some smashed banana, he pretended to warm his hands on her ass and put five dollars down.

'That's a nice little pussy you got there. Give it a shake.'

Frankie picked up the money and raised Tiger high in the air.

Quohog pushed a dime into the Wurlitzer and 'La Grange' came on.

'Give em a bump,' he said.

The fat riff filled the space and Frankie kissed the cat on the nose and spun around. Quohog hooted his appreciation and humped a chair. The way he was laughing lit a fuse in my head so I grabbed Frankie by the arm and she knocked into the jukebox scraping the needle across the record.

The cat dropped to the floor and ran off to hide behind the jukebox.

Frankie turned. 'You don't own me, Turner,' she said. 'Look what you done. You scared Tiger.'

Quohog sat spread legged in front of us with a shit eating grin.

'You want to keep that girl on a string,' he said.

Frankie slapped the five-dollar bill down on top of his inky head. Quohog stood up and the bill slid from his bald crown and see-sawed gently down to the floor. The snakes on his arm flexed long and lean as he grabbed Frankie hard between the legs and pushed her back, slamming her head against the wall.

'You little cunt.'

*

I moved fast and low. Driving my fist so hard into the greaser's groin that the punk bent double and puked. I did a little war dance but waited too long and Quohog stood back up and smashed his knuckles into the side of my skull and slammed me into the ground

46

where I curled into a ball and waited for the beating to stop. I could hear the dull thump of his hands landing on me. Coloured lights flashed in my head. I crawled under a table and he started in with his feet. I heard my jaw crack, and felt the blood trickle down the back of my throat, the taste on my tongue like a bad penny.

Next thing I knew, Millboy was stood there holding that replica pistol so tight his knuckles were bone white and shaking. In the faded light of the Neon D, the pistol looked real all right.

Nobody moved.

Janice Morningstar had a phone in her hand.

'You'd better all just go,' she said. 'You better all just leave.'

I rolled out from beneath the table. My jaw ached and felt lop-sided. When I tried to speak I slobbered.

'You heard what she said.'

Quohog stared curiously at the pistol and put his hands up in mock surrender. Millboy walked Quohog out and Frankie pocketed the five bill and started wiping the blood off the side of my face with a napkin.

'Don't blame Tiger,' she said.

My head rang like a bell. 'I thought she was a good luck cat?' I said.

'Think about what could have happened if she hadn't been here.'

'Maybe my ear would still be attached to the side of my head.'

Janice Morningstar was straightening the chairs when Millboy came running back. One eye rolling around, looking for me.

'I just stabbed him in the head.'

'Stabbed who?' I said.

'Quohog.'

'What do you mean?' I said.

'I just stabbed Quohog.'

'Where?'

'In the head.'

'I mean, where is he?'

'He's twisting around in the parking lot. Holding his neck and complaining.'

Through the misty rain I saw a giant neon coffee cup with a handle shaped like a D. Under the illuminated letter Quohog was slumped with his hand clamped over the back of his skull. Blood oozed from between his fingers and splattered on the concrete in big, shiny, red stars. The knife stuck out of his head like a clockwork key.

'Oh man,' I said. 'What have you done?'

'I stabbed him in the head,' Millboy said again. 'It was an accident.'

'You stabbed him in the head by accident?'

Quohog was gurgling up blood. It was bubbling on his lips and his eyes were bulging. Frankie came out sucking on a Ring Pop and put the cat down.

'What happened?'

'Millboy stabbed him in the head,' I said.

'By accident,' Millboy chipped in. 'He took out a knife and we started to wrestle. Started to fight. Everything got messed up.'

Tiger lapped from the pool of blood that was leaking out of Quohog's head. Frankie picked the cat back up. 'Gross,' she said. 'What are we going to do now?'

We shunted the greaser facedown onto the backseat, careful not to dislodge the knife. The whole time he was moaning. Me and Frankie squeezed onto the passenger side as Millboy shoved the gearshift into drive.

The car pitched forward with a jerk.

Millboy restarted the engine but kept it running at standstill. 'He pulled out a knife and we started wrestling,' he said. 'Somehow his arm got all twisted up and the knife got stuck in his head.'

'Are you worried he might be dead?' I said.

'Not really. I didn't kill him. It was an accident.'

'You accidently killed him,' Frankie said.

'Exactly,' Millboy said. 'It wasn't my fault.'

'I'm not dead,' someone said.

We turned around and Quohog was sitting up straight. His face looked like someone had thrown a can of red paint over it and his eyes were like two white walnuts busting through his skull. He reached up to pull the knife out, and the hole made a sucking sound like dregs going down a sinkhole. For a moment it seemed like he'd be okay. Then a stream of blood fountained and fell across his face like a thick red veil as a strong odour filled the car, reminding me of autumn.

Wet leaves and bonfires.

Quohog leaned forward and stretched his arms out toward us.

'Jesus Christ,' he said. 'Oh God. Please help me. Jesus Christ.'

It was like he was awake for the first time in his life.

The electric tubes of the Neon D lit up the inside of the car with a dreamlike luminosity. Quohog thrashed wildly splashing us with gore. Frankie was shrieking. Tiger was leaping around. Millboy hit the gearshift but had left the handbrake on and the car edged slowly forward tyres screeching.

In the madness I could see Janice Morningstar standing in the doorframe – her hand over her mouth and her eyes wide with panic. Millboy cut the engine and Quohog buckled between the seats like a pile of dirty washing.

The forces that throw you together can also tear you apart. For the last month we'd been living in each other's space. Sharing beds and smokes. Now we were driving a stolen car with a dead Hell's Angel on the backseat and a trunk full of unreliable dictionaries. None of it was our fault, or maybe it all was. I didn't have to take that job with Romeo and Frankie didn't have to slap that five down on top of Quohog's head. But like old Carpenter said about that poem by Mr. Robert Frost.

We took the road less travelled, and now we were fucked.

PART TWO

Into This World
We're Thrown

THE SUMMERHOUSE

Maybe we should have turned back but there didn't seem much point so we just kept on because we didn't know what else to do. There were some tapes in the footwell and Frankie changed cassettes until she found one that sounded like rolling thunder. As the song played, Frankie took Quohog's five-dollar bill and lit it with a match and we watched as the edges curled and the smoke snaked up across the roof, drifting like a small black cloud.

'Kathy Lee showed me how to do this,' she said.

'An invocation of demons,' Millboy said. 'Sorcery of some kind.'

Frankie crushed the bill in her hand and opened the window and held her arm out for a moment, bringing it back and showing us her open palm as if it were a black wound or some reminder of what Quohog had done to her.

'Gone with the wind,' she said.

'Amen,' Millboy said.

Frankie drew a black cross on Millboy's brow with the cinders and jammed the replica pistol against his head. 'You're my hero, Randy. You saved Turner and me. When we get a chance, we'll dump the pig and just keep going.'

We sped on through the night.

Like a light box flickering in the dark.

To stay awake we told each other stories. I wanted to go travelling. To see some of the places I'd only read about. We dreamed of a future that ignored the past. Frankie was applying for college but was behind on the work.

'Seventeen with parental consent and I'll be that in February,' she said. 'Just need to get that grade ten. I can't stand the thought of living in that apartment another year and working for Romeo, selling dictionaries and lightbulbs and some such shit. School is the only way out for me.'

Millboy said, 'Look at the three of us. Don't tell me that's an accident. I could have gotten killed, but fate turned around Quohog's hand and he ended up stabbing himself in the neck. The Almighty got plans for me and I'm looking forward to em.'

Frankie took Millboy's hand and traced the contours of his palm and read the fate-line like it was all written out by decree. 'There's a light inside of you,' she said. 'There's a greatness inside of this boy.'

Algonquin Park rose up like a mystic forest.

*

Millboy told us about the Cree – about how they had lived in Canada for eight thousand years before any white man arrived. He told us about a flesh-eating demon called the Wendigo that dwelt in the woods. He said that many hunters and backpackers had gone missing over the years. Others had been possessed by the Wendigo spirit. He told us about someone who'd shown up in town claiming his wife and kids were missing. When the soldiers got to the camp they'd found broken skulls and snapped bones with the marrow sucked out. Half-eaten carcasses. Buckets of blood. Clumps of hair. He said that a person had murdered his entire family and cooked their flesh. He said that a person can go crazy in the frozen north.

'How do you know this stuff?' I said.

'I've been doing some research,' Millboy said. 'My great grandmother was a full-blown Cree and fought alongside braves at the Battle of Cut Knife. That's why I'm so small. After the war she married a soldier with bowlegs and that gift is still rattling around the tubes.'

*

The first flakes fell soft and silent and decorated the fields like white linen. Up ahead a lone star shone in the night. We followed that star and followed the tracks made by other cars until there were no other tracks and no other cars left to follow. Overtaken by tiredness, I went off road and passed some feral horses that stood pale in the moonlight. Up ahead, a solitary cabin that looked like something a child might draw: a small-framed house, remote and off road, surrounded by tall trees and next to a lake with a knoll that led up into the woods. Seemingly deserted, it would at least give us shelter for the night.

There were no cars parked, so we tramped through the snow and broke a glass panel in the backdoor and stamped the drift from our shoes.

Inside was homely and dark, and some dead bugs that decorated the sills now moved in the draft that blew in through the broken window. A dull bulb hung from a cord. There was a tea kettle and coffee pot and the cutlery draw seemed fusty and rank, but the electricity was still hooked up, so Millboy turned on the stove and removed his wet runners and sat on a kitchen chair with his feet in the oven. The stink coming off his socks like rotten food.

'Are we robbing this place?' he said.

'No one lives here,' I said. 'We're just looking after it for them.'

'Housesitting,' Millboy said. 'They should be paying us.'

LAKE OF FIRE

It couldn't have been more than an hour since we left the Neon D, but it already seemed like a world away. I should have known there was a reason why Romeo sent us to make the pickup rather than go himself. Quohog taking that blade and getting stabbed in the process told me as much. Millboy always said he had the strength of two people on account of him absorbing the spirit of his dead twin. Maybe there was something in that. Or maybe there was something else. But what chance created the circumstance for Millboy to always get into trouble and out of it too? Ever since he was a foetus about to be terminated that seemed to be the way of things. He was a stranger to me and yet my best friend.

The summerhouse was built from a wood frame, but had been

neglected. Water came in at the windows and the gardens had run wild. It looked like the family who'd once lived there were now passed on and the children grown up with families of their own. The letters and postcards I found were all ancient and addressed to the Nunleys.

There were photographs too.

Some men holding a big catch of pike after a fishing adventure next to a big old Chev Nomad. Assorted dogs. Two boys dressed the same – red-faced and goofy. One picture taken right out front when the house was full of love and the paint brand new. The house had seen birthdays, anniversaries, and maybe even funerals. That's just the natural order of things.

All families grow apart or fall away from each other in the end.

Millboy said he knew of a family who were so close that they all lived together in the same house even when the kids grew up. The brother and sister with an unnatural devotion to each other taking on the reverse role of mother and father when the parents got senile and had to wear diapers.

*

The summerhouse may have been abandoned, but the kitchen was well stocked with packets of dried foodstuffs. We feasted on canned peaches and cereal, and then ransacked the upstairs rooms and dressed in the Nunleys' clothes and built a fire and got the record player working. The three of us dancing around the room to someone called Jim Reeves.

Adios amigo, adios my friend.

Morning was breaking and a ray of light bust through a crack in the heavy curtains by the time me and Frankie went upstairs to the bedroom. You couldn't hear a thing, or you could hear everything, depending on your point of view.

Just the speed of the wind and a bird calling out a high sweet whistle.

We sank into the soft mattress and looked at a ceramic frog playing a trumpet. We kicked off our jeans and took off our shirts and laid in just our underwear. The heat from our bodies like a fever as we lay listening to the sound of each other breathing.

Too tired to sleep and high on adrenaline, Frankie started talking.

'I can't ever remember a time when he lived at home,' she said. 'He must have left long ago. I have a memory, but I don't know if it's real or fake. There's a photograph of Kathy Lee holding me and looking like the happiest girl in the world. The way she's gazing into that camera. It could only have been him taking the photograph. That's the closest thing to a family picture I've got.'

I ran my fingers over the bracelet of white scars that twisted around her wrist and felt myself sinking into the deep hollow of sleep. I grasped at words and tried to form a sentence but was unable to stay awake and slept like the dead.

*

When I awoke it was near dark and I had a hammer in my head. Millboy was leaning over me holding that Zippo with the blue flame curling around his thumb.

'Get up, Turner,' he said. 'There's a car outside.'

I walked over to the window and tried to focus. In the near distance you could see some taillights blinking orange.

I rubbed my eyes. 'Where's our car?' I said.

Millboy said, 'That is our car.'

In the deathly quiet of the night the horn blasted and Frankie sat up screaming, which made me and Miller scream and grab on to each other like a couple of fools. As the horn died to a whine we stood staring out the window waiting for someone to get out the Maverick but nobody did, so I pulled on my jeans and boots and wrapped myself up in some blankets before going outside while the others got dressed.

*

When I got to the car, Quohog was face down on the steering wheel, congealed blood hung down from his neck like a black rope. I turned the engine off and pushed him back on the seat. His fat head limp and a giant Q inked on top of his dome. Millboy came over wearing Mrs. Nunley's fur coat and two hats.

'Must have been a death rattle,' he said. 'Like when a chicken gets its head cut off and runs around.'

'He was driving a car,' I said. 'Ever seen a chicken drive a car?'

'Well, he's dead now,' Millboy said.

'He looked dead this morning,' I said.

The three of us hauled Quohog onto a bedsheet and carried him as if he were in a sack. Even in the freezing cold, he stunk, so we decided to bury him.

Millboy fetched a spade from the woodshed but the ground was frozen solid.

Frankie said, 'What are we going to do now?'

'The lake,' Millboy said. 'Let's dump him in the lake.'

We dragged him through the snow as if he were a bag of potatoes and then rested him on the jetty where he slid halfway into the water.

Millboy said, 'Put him in one of those boats.'

We swung Quohog around in the water and tried to heave him over the side and managed to get his head and shoulders over, but his gut was the problem as it bowed under the keel, so I took the rope from the anchor and tied it around his feet and worked out a way of reeling him in like a big fish. Quohog upended and hit the deck. The boat rocked and some water washed in as he lay with his tattooed head framed by the bow and his face lit by a starry night. There were white icicles on Quohog's eyelashes and his lips had turned deep blue. Small black leeches gripped his forehead.

He was an ugly bastard all right.

In that time Millboy had gone and come back carrying a metal can.

'Kerosene,' he said. 'They use it to refill Zippos. There's a stack of it in the woodshed.'

I walked around the jetty, overgrown with long grass. Pushed under the slipway and tangled up in reeds was another boat. I pulled it free and we climbed down, rowing out and pulling Quohog behind. When we got to the middle of the lake, Millboy poured in the kerosene, soaking Quohog with fuel before throwing in the empty can.

Frankie clapped her hands together. 'Maybe we should say something?'

In the light of the big moon Randy Miller stood up and held that Zippo at arm's length as if he were the Statue of Liberty. Then he tossed the flame into the boat where it lit up with a whoosh.

'Smoke on the water,' he yelled. 'Fire in the sky.'

The blaze roared with such fierceness that I couldn't look. Around the parameter of the lake you could see the red eyes of ducks, and beneath the water the black shapes of strange fish. The bare branches of trees shaped crooked against the night sky and I felt the skin on my face blister as we watched Quohog rise up in the middle of the boat with his arms outstretched like a fiery cross before falling back into the water leaving the boat smouldering on the surface of the lake.

THE SPIRIT BOARD

It is at this point my memory turns out to be unreliable and so becomes a mix of fact and fiction. If what happened next seems too fantastical to believe, then know that it at least happened, as what follows is a blur – a dream – some long-forgotten memory of a walk through a hall of mirrors. It is true that we drank home-made liquor, and it is true that we ate what was left of the canned peaches and dried bread. But it is also true that we felt a presence of what I consider to be a wicked and malevolent spirit.

After I rebuilt the fire, Frankie lit some candles and took the plastic letters from a Scrabble board and placed them around the edge of the table. Then she took two coasters and flipped em over. She wrote YES on one, and NO on the other, before placing them on opposite sides of the board. Millboy looked uneasy about the whole thing.

'Is this some more of that belly dancer stuff?' he said.

'We need help,' Frankie said. 'We can ask relatives for advice.'

'Gramps wouldn't know what to do,' Millboy said.

'Dead ones,' Frankie said. 'Not the living ones.'

'Maybe you can ask Elvis,' I said.

I knew Kathy Lee messed around with picture cards and spirit boards and that Frankie supposed it was true, so we sat cross-legged and pushed the shot glass around the table and asked it dumb questions.

I must admit that I treated the whole thing like a joke, but at some point, it stopped being funny and the room grew smaller, softer; the light dimmer. Our faces twisted in the candleflame – Millboy as a blackbird: Frankie the wolf, Tiger morphed into a snake, coiled in the fireplace as the sparks danced like fireflies before turning to dust.

I lay on my side opposite Millboy who lay the other way around – our heads aligned, and we stared into each other's eyes as if they were portals into another world. The dark circles under his eyes became his eyebrows while his eyebrows became the dark circles under his eyes. I felt detached from my body. Set free from my physical form. Like I was floating around the room observing everything at once. Frankie wanted to know about her future. The past. She put her finger back on top of the tumbler and told us to do the same.

'Fuck this witchy poo shit,' Millboy said. 'I'm not doing it no more.'

It was like a compulsion, and the more we fed it the stronger it got.

The glass started moving again. Slowly then faster. We raced it around the table. It seemed to have an energy all of its own. Every time we asked a question the answer came back as a riddle. We were still moving the glass except we weren't. I mean we weren't moving it, something else was. At one point we lifted our fingers but the glass kept spelling out words:

Hell.

Mad.

Knife.

It spelled out the word, REQUIEM.

I asked if anyone knew what requiem meant and no one did, so I went outside and took a dictionary from the back of the car.

In the bone white of a winter's moon, the mountains were black and the sounds of the forest spoke to me through the trees. I don't know how long I stood outside, but when I went back the two of them were sitting with their arms around each other.

I took the book and flicked back and forth until I found the page and then the word. Next to it an illustration of a hooded figure knelt at an altar. Three people stood over him. One reading a book. I traced my finger under the words and read out loud: 'It says here, Mass for the Souls of the Dead.'

Frankie wrapped the blanket tight around her face and skipped around the room speaking in rhymes. 'The power of three,' she said. 'We are three.'

My eyeballs started trembling. My skin fizzed. It felt like something had poisoned me. The glass was still moving on its own. Millboy had the face of an old man when he spoke. I had to keep reminding myself he was just sixteen.

'There is a dark angel in this house,' he said. 'An angel of death.'

Frankie cradled Millboy in her arms as if she were comforting an infant.

'Hush-a-bye. Don't you cry.'

The glass started to tremble and then exploded into a heap of crystalized shards.

Whatever had possessed us, was now gone.

Frankie took Millboy's hands and turned him around as if they were dancing to a tune only they could hear. I watched them curiously as they swayed. They had the strangeness of twins. One the mirror of the other. My blood rushed hot as I moved in-between them. The three of us danced together. We danced into the hallway, up the stairs and into the bedroom. Unable to tell one from the other and so out of our minds that I can't even remember what happened next except that it felt like the most natural thing in the world.

*

When I woke up, Millboy and Frankie were asleep under Mrs. Nunley's fur coat. I went to the bathroom and emptied my guts down the pan and puked up my insides. I drank some cold water from the tap but still felt nauseous. The stink of kerosene on my clothes reminding me of what had happened. When I went outside to get some fresh air, I saw Janice Morningstar stood in the daylight holding a basket of groceries.

'I thought you might want something to eat,' she said.

JANICE MORNINGSTAR

That morning found us miserable and ready to go home. I think all three of us had thrown up or had the shits or both. Millboy was the whitest person I ever saw. Blue veins running under his thin skin. Ribcage sticking out like one of them famine relief posters. It looked as if he was wearing a pair of Gramps' underpants. The leg holes so big his balls kept falling out. Janice Morningstar stared at him.

'Don't mind me,' she said. 'I got brothers.'

'Must have been them peaches,' Millboy said. 'Anyone check the use by date? I feel hollowed out. Slightly shaky, but born again and ready for a new day. How'd you find us anyhow?'

Janice Morningstar put the groceries down and said, 'Followed you for a while, and then lost you. Saw the smoke and guessed it was you and knew it was when I saw that Ford Maverick ditched in the lane. What happened to that knife you stuck in his head?'

'It was an accident,' Millboy said.

'Where's Quohog?' Janice Morningstar said.

I thought about Quohog suspended like a cooked pig under the lake less than fifty yards away. Unsure of Janice Morningstar's relationship with Romeo and the bikers, I lied.

'We left him in the car to sleep it off. Must have hitched a ride back to town.'

Janice Morningstar looked at me with an expression that said you're full of shit and said, 'You're full of shit. Looks like you hauled something from the car to that lake over there. What with the smoke and all, I'd say there's been a cremation.'

'It was just a pickup and drop off job,' I said. 'This wasn't supposed to happen.'

'Well they'll be looking for their comrade soon enough, and that means the Devil's Children will be looking for you. Where's the knife?'

'It's in the car as far as I know,' I said.

The four of us tramped over to the Maverick and I cranked open the backdoor. It swung loose on its hinges and a dust of snow collapsed. Inside was rank and a cluster of winter fleas and stink bugs had collected into the corners where the blood had clotted and turned into something resembling frozen jelly.

We scrubbed the vinyl with some pages ripped from the dictionaries and brushed out the dirty snow but couldn't find the knife anywhere.

'It must have fallen out,' Millboy said. 'Either that or might still be in the parking lot of the Neon D.'

Frankie said, 'More likely Quohog still has it.'

'In his head?' Janice Morningstar said.

'It was an accident,' Millboy said. 'He did it to himself.'

We dug out around the car and laid some brushwood so that we could reverse out. Then we scraped the ice off the windshield and found some tyre chains in the trunk and fitted them to the wheels and drove up and down the lane a few times so that the track was good and we could at least get to the highway if supplies were needed. Within the hour we were eating hard boiled eggs and waffles and washing them down with hot coffee.

Millboy asked about the Wendigo. About whether it was safe to go into the woods. Janice Morningstar dangled an eggshell off her thumbnail and flipped it around. 'The atoosh is a cannibal spirit that can turn a human into a killer,' she said. 'Even a little punk like you.'

'What do you mean?' Millboy said.

'Anyone can become a Wendigo,' Janice Morningstar said. 'It's not so hard to understand. There's no monster in the forest waiting. It's inside of you.'

'Inside me?' Millboy said.

Janice Morningstar said, 'What is it you're so afraid of that you start to think the only way to stop the horror is to destroy the thing that's making you afraid. But before long, it starts to control you. Whispering in your ear, so that you don't even know who you are or what to think anymore. Scraping away everything until you become a hollow thing. And when you become a hollow thing, that's when the atoosh starts to live in your head.'

'Crock of shit,' I said. 'Myths and legends from a fuckin waffle waitress.'

'No, it's not,' Millboy said. 'Look what we did last night.'

'Shut up, Miller,' I said.

'I know what you did last night,' Janice Morningstar said. 'You messed up. That knife was the deal Romeo made with the Devil's Children. Do you understand? That's what you were supposed to pick up. It's a relic – a silver dagger that used to belong to a chief. What you might call an antique worth money and more than that. The Children were looting from indigenous graves, dealing in stolen native artefacts. Romeo was selling them on and making a profit.'

'Quohog pulled a knife on me,' Millboy said. 'He tried to kill me.'

'He wasn't pulling it on you,' Janice Morningstar said. 'He was trying to give it to you. But you got frightened and took it and stabbed him in the neck. Something just took over and you went with it. I've heard of people who, when they look in the mirror, don't even recognise themselves anymore. They stand gazing at their own reflection as if they're remembering a dream from a long time ago. Trying to remember if it's real or a nightmare. Every action takes you further away from the place you really want to be. You get lost quick.'

'How do you get back from that place?' I said.

'How would I know?' Janice Morningstar said. 'I'm just a waffle waitress.'

THE HUT IN THE WOODS

It snowed for days and then rained all night so that the snow turned into a dirty slop that soaked your feet right through and then it snowed again. Lost in the flow of time we played games and kept the fire strong until the house was cooking like an oven. Janice was in the kitchen slicing onions and tossing pieces of meat to Tiger when Frankie came in and drew a heart on the wall.

'Anytime you can think of something worth remembering, write it on the wall,' she said. 'And if you can't write it, draw a picture.'

Janice Morningstar picked up the marker pen and drew the frame of the summerhouse. Then she dipped her hands in some sauce and painted her palms around the frame and said, 'I like to make art with material objects, animal bones and other things

I find on the road. I glue them to boards in different shapes and paint around them, maybe give them names.'

Frankie said, 'What kind of names?'

'It depends on how I feel. I wanted to go to art school but my mother needed me at home. But she's free now and so am I.'

Frankie said, 'What do you mean?'

Janice Morningstar said, 'My mother got sick and didn't get better. Her skin turned yellow and what was left of her hair fell out. She didn't even know who I was at the end. I said, Mother, do you know who I am? And she just looked at me like I was a stranger and said, I want to go home. You are going home, I said. Am I? she said. Yes, I said. And meant that too. Only not in the way she thought. My mother left these shores and just drifted. Never came back. Soon as the doctor gave us the diagnosis, it was like she was in God's own waiting room. As the days slipped away so did she. Just lay there surrounded by the junk she'd accumulated her whole life. Her wedding dress still hung in the closet even though the old man left years ago. First thing I did when she died was burn it. Second thing I did was leave school and get a job. If it wasn't for the Native Resource Centre, I would have starved.'

'Is that how you ended up working at the Neon D?' Frankie said.

'Only until I make enough selling my art. Not the stuff you buy in giftshops. I'm not interested in selling dreamcatchers to day-trippers.'

'Does Romeo know who you are?' Frankie said. 'What about the Angels?'

Tiger was climbing up Janice Morningstar's jeans trying to claw at a piece of spaghetti. 'They know who I am,' she said. 'But they don't know what I am. They use the Neon D as a trading post and think they can just take what is sacred and sell it on to rich folk in high-rise apartments downtown, but they do not know what they are dealing with. That knife will find its way back home and you're going to help me.'

The piled-up firewood was nearly all gone so me and Millboy went gathering sticks and just to get out of the way generally. We had a canvas bag and crammed it full of brushwood and dragged it around the perimeter of the lake.

We tramped through the snow over to the jetty where smears of blood still stained the ice. A pall of smoke hung over the boat and some red winged birds perched on the now burned out frame – their crimson badges flashing brilliant in the midday sun. Nobody mentioned Quohog. Nobody mentioned the knife. But we were both thinking on it.

Millboy said, 'We'll just have to wait for the lake to thaw. Maybe come back in the summer.'

Ice was forming around the shallows and working its way toward the centre. I tested the ice with my foot. 'It'll freeze over and the crabs will eat what's left,' I said.

'The lake contains bad spirits,' Millboy said. 'Trapped by the frost. When it thaws, the atoosh will come.'

'You don't really believe all that stuff?' I said.

'I don't disbelieve it,' he said.

Neither did I.

*

We reached the top of the hill and stopped to catch our breath. Smoke curled up from the summerhouse and marked us out as the only people for miles. It may have been the wind, or it may have been the rocks, but from where we stood, it was if all the clamour of the land was to be found in the hollow of that valley. We walked deeper into the woods, the undergrowth so dense our voices became hushed. Our sense of self sharpened by the sense of space.

Eventually we came to a small clearing. Nestled into the vegetation like some fairy tale home to a witch was a door. I brushed the snow from the handle but the lock was frozen. Millboy struck a match and held the burn under the bolt and the door opened and we stepped into a hut just big enough for the two of us. There were some newspapers scattered around. Millboy pushed some loose pages into an empty can to make a fire and we watched as the liquid paint flared sapphire blue – the sting of the smoke burning in our nostrils.

Millboy wouldn't look me in the eye. 'Are we homos?' he said.

'I don't think so,' I said.

'But what happened that night we played the Spirit Board?'

I finished the sentence for him. 'Doesn't mean a thing.'

'I caught Frankie looking at us,' Millboy said.

'I don't even know what you're talking about,' I said.

'I don't feel ashamed or dirty,' Millboy said. 'It's like we were drunk on something.'

*

Outside the hut the day had fallen away as the light from the moon fused with the crystals, turning the whole landscape into a kind of dreamland. Columns of red and green shimmered in the valley while silvery orbs floated like Chinese lanterns. In the distance, the windows of the house lit up dark blue. In the peaceful quiet of the winterlight, we freewheeled down the hill, skidding on the heels of our boots, walking carefully around the lake and back toward the house. Cold sweat prickling on the back of my neck.

Ice cracking underfoot like thin panes of glass.

THE BOOKSELLERS

We were out of money so decided to do some bookselling. With it being the holiday season, a lot of offices had already closed, so we drove out of town to the suburbs to be met by a washed-out wasteland of half-empty buildings and garages. We trawled the industrial estates looking for likely terrain and an easy make. There was a three-story building that looked promising. Through the windows you could see clerks, typists and administrators, all going about their business. A few cars were parked up:

Pintos, Toyotas, and a Ducati Scrambler chained to a post.

We pulled over and told Janice to keep the engine running while we considered a plan. Frankie always made the most sales so she would go in first to give us the best chance of making any money.

Me and Millboy hit separate floors. It had been a few months since we last worked and I was a little nervous and out of practice. I tried to remember the lines and went over them in my head and then snorted some speed Millboy had laid out in nasty lines on the dash.

We waited for the doorkeeper to go for a smoke, and then fast-walked in through the building with the Merriam-Webster's held high like they were some kind of certificate of legitimate entry. Straight away my adrenaline started pumping and I sprang up the stairs and walked into an open plan office only to be met by an uninterested typist who looked at me curiously.

I held up the dictionary and forgot my lines.

'Yes,' she said, 'how can I help?'

I had made this pitch a hundred times before, but right then it felt like my mouth was full of cotton wool. 'We have an incredible offer on these illustrated encyclopaedic dictionaries. These Merriam-Webster books will cost you fifty dollars downtown, but I can do you a deal today, and that means for just twenty dollars, you get to own this exclusive unique edition leather-bound book that comes complete with a luxury box and a lifetime money back guarantee.'

I didn't sound convincing. She didn't look convinced.

'Why aren't you in school?' she said.

I blundered an apology and felt my face flush as I put the book back in the box. Over in the corner some dogeared tinsel hung from the threadbare branches of a Christmas tree that was mostly wire. Somewhere a radio played:

Our finest gifts we bring, Pa Rum Pum Pum Pum.

An old guy stepped out of a room and told me to follow him into his office, where he closed the door. The radiators were on full and the windows were all steamed up. The office stank of body odour and tobacco. He had one of those faces you might describe as kindly. Soft around the edges. He said his name was Farley. He smoked a pipe and when he took it out of his mouth, he licked his lips with the tip of his tongue and chuckled to himself.

'You got a name, son?'

I thought about this for a moment and then lied like I always did. 'John Turner.'

'Well, it's nice to meet you, John.'

'It's very nice to meet you too, Farley.'

'So, what are you doing all the way out here, John. Where do you come from? Where do you live?'

'Came up from Toronto. Working on a job and staying out by the lake.'

'You drove all this way north to sell books to typists? You're not from the city. Where are you from?'

'You wouldn't have heard of it,' I said. 'A small town far away.'

'Well,' Farley said. "Toronto has it all. Blacks. Portuguese. Chinese. Scottish. People go there to start again. Lots of construction work.'

'I moved to the city with my father at the start of the year after my parents broke up. I'm just trying to make a few dollars so I can go home and see my mother.'

Farley knocked the burning embers out of his pipe into a bowl and stuffed it full of fresh tobacco with his nicotine stained thumb. 'That's your pitch right there,' he said. 'Just tell the girls in the office that, and they'll all buy a book off of you. You won't have to talk all that nonsense then.'

Farley was trying to humiliate me. Or maybe he was trying to help. I don't know. I told him the books were garbage. That they were destined for the pulp machine, but somehow ended up in a warehouse where they were sold as a job lot to market traders trying to make a few dollars downtown. I'm not sure if he was impressed or if he just felt sorry for me, but he picked up the book and flicked through a few pages before setting it down again.

'I appreciate your honesty,' he said. 'I don't know why or how you ended up trying to sell spoiled merchandise to good people, but when I saw you out in the office, you looked like the one being fooled not them. You might not have the best job in the world right now, but you're working and that's nothing to be ashamed of. Do you understand?'

'Yes, sir.'

Everyone has to make a living. Have you got anything to hide, John?'

'Not me, sir,' I said, but stuttered, and Farley said, 'Go on.'

'Well, everybody's got something to hide,' I said.

'Do you follow the Jesus way?'

'I believe and fear the Angels,' I said. 'It's like I can almost feel their presence.'

Farley put down a twenty-dollar bill and picked up the book.

'You know what Saint Paul said? That there may well be Angels in our midst, and we should be careful how we treat each other.'

I took the money and left the dictionary on the table.

When I walked past the typist she was on the phone and still looking at me. There was a leather jacket on the back of her chair and a motorcycle helmet under the desk. I didn't think much of it at the time, but it must have been her Ducati Scrambler outside.

When I got back to the car, Frankie was empty-handed but Millboy was still holding onto his book. We counted out forty dollars and split it four ways. The security guard was making his way over. Waving a clipboard and getting ready to bawl us out. Millboy was gearing up to give him a mouthful back, but I stopped him right there.

'He's just doing his job,' I said. 'Everyone's got to make a living. Might not be the best job in the world right now, but that's nothing to be ashamed of.'

The guard rapped on the window and pointed at a sign above the entrance that said *No Hawkers, Agents or Canvassers*.

'Do you understand what that means?' he said.

I opened the window and gave him Millboy's dictionary. Webster's finest.

THE DEVIL'S CHILDREN

The snow had begun to fall again. It capped the fenceposts and iced up the windows and blustered in through the damaged door and then melted away leaving wet patches on the rug. We were out of wood but Millboy had found an electric fire in one of the rooms and the stink of burning dust came off as the hot bars spat in the cold air. The room had been decorated with paper streamers and a small silvery tree now stood on top of the radiogram. A few baubles hung, and some festive cards were draped over a cotton thread that was pinned above the fireplace. Santa Claus in a flying saucer.

Seasons' Greetings to Mr. and Mrs. Nunley.

With the money from the dictionary sales we'd been able to buy fresh food and supplies: cigarettes and beer. Millboy inhaled on an Export A and blew a perfect circle of smoke. 'There ought to be more days like this,' he said. 'These are the best days.'

Frankie said, 'You know, we could fix it up and make it home.'

'Why not?' I said. 'No one else lives here.'

'We live here,' Millboy said. 'It's our place now and we'll do what we want with it.'

In those weeks we had become a family. I had feelings for Frankie that I never had for anybody else and she felt the same way too. It was as if the household had a personality and influence over us. Benign yet watchful.

We took the clothes from the wardrobes and read the books from the shelves. We listened to old records and even gazed upon the personal letters addressed to people we never knew. Harmless phantoms in every room – watching us as if trying to remember who we were.

Preoccupied with this thought, I had not noticed that Millboy had gone quiet. Now sat at the window rubbing at the condensation with the heel of his hand and staring out into the darkness.

'That don't look natural to me,' he said. 'Come take a look.'

I wandered over and pressed my face up to the glass.

There was a rumble of exhausts as some motorbikes appeared. Silvery columns of fumes materialising like spirits in the night. Four dark figures stood their bikes and shook the frost from their long leather coats.

Millboy said, 'Looks like Angels to me.'

'The Devil's Children,' Frankie said.

'They've come looking for Quohog,' I said.

'The Duke,' Janice Morningstar said. 'He's come for the knife.'

We went out the backdoor and ran down the track. The moon like a blue lamp casting a wide circle of light across the fields. Our breath turning to frost.

White horses watching from across the way.

Tiger, stuffed in a handbag.

The greasers stormed the house, ripping the place apart and driving their bikes into the living area. From the track we could hear the sound of motorcycles echoing across the lake like loons. We started the Maverick and drove with the headlights off. Just when we thought it was safe to turn the lights back on, some orange spots burned through the rear window and the bikes came roaring up, funneling us off onto a slip road where we hit some low hanging branches and skidded to a stop.

One of the bikers stood on his saddle and stomped on the trunk before unclipping a chain from his waist. He began to bludgeon the rear window. The glass warped and shattered. The biker took out his dong and started to urinate. Great arcs of piss flooded the backseat. We got out and ran.

Into the woods.

The motorcycles scrambled between the trees. Lamps like searchlights. One of em held a flare – his exhaust backfiring. I reached out for Frankie but the lead rider had pulled her over the gas tank while another had Janice by the hair and was dragging her through the snow in circles.

Something hit me and I went down.

When I came around I was hurting all over. The girls were gone. Two greasers stood over me. One had a bright orange beard and wore flying goggles. The other sported a spiked helmet and struck me hard across the side of the head with a leather glove.

'Where's Quohog?' he said.

'I don't know.'

'Where's the knife?'

'What knife?'

He hit me again. 'We found Quohog's cycle outside the Neon D.'

I rubbed the side of my head. 'You'd better ask Romeo.'

'Why?'

'Romeo showed up at the Neon D the same night and told us he was taking care of business himself. Said we should go home. Him and Quohog went off together in that English Jag and that's the last I saw of em.'

'So how come you ran?'

'We didn't run, we just kept driving. Where's Frankie?'

The bright orange beard pointed a fat oily finger at me.

'With that squaw and we'll get the truth out of them.'

The motorcycles disappeared into the whiteout. Miller's face was smashed open again. I cleaned him up best I could and cracked his nose back into place. He didn't thank me.

Brittle with cold, we wrapped up in everything we could find and sat in the car. It got so that I couldn't feel the ends of my fingers and my toes felt like they had disappeared. On the backseat, the bag with Tiger jerked around like a Mexican jumping bean. There was a house just down and opposite with a woman in the yard. Millboy went back to the Maverick and took the last dictionary from the trunk and crossed over and knocked the door.

The woman came out and I could see them talking but couldn't hear what they were saying, although she kept looking over and nodding her head as if in agreement with whatever lie he was spinning. When Millboy came back he was carrying a bag of road salt and a shovel. I took the spade and started digging around the Maverick.

'What did you say to that woman?' I said.

'That you were my brother and that you were a drug addict.'

'You said I was a drug addict?'

'And violent.'

'You said I was a violent drug addict?'

Millboy scattered the salt along the track. 'I told her we had to get your prescription methadone before the drugstore closed for New Year, otherwise you might get sick. She pointed to my nose and asked if you did that and I said you did.'

'I just reset it for you.'

'I didn't lie. You take drugs and you bust my nose.'

'I'm not your brother,' I said.

By the time we fixed the tyre and got back to the summerhouse it was getting dark all over again. The Children had wrecked Janice Morningstar's car – torched and dumped, smoking in a ditch.

Frankie lay upstairs in the tub. Her eyes a washed out grey, finger bruises over her pale white body. Through the soapy water I could see red circles lacing their way up to the surface.

'Where's Tiger?' she said.

'She's all right,' I said. 'How about you?'

'I got stomach cramps,' she said. 'Feels like somebody pulled out my insides and stuffed em back again.'

Janice was in the doorway. The side of her face like a purple balloon all swollen up. 'They took us to a motel in White River and got us high,' she said. 'The Duke got the White River Motelier to take pictures of Frankie out of her mind on something before dumping us back here.'

*

Later that night Frankie and Janice were in bed talking, I was reading. Millboy was on the floor, breathing so quiet he could have been dead. But then he sat bolt upright and shrieking with his eyes wide open and turned his head like that scene in *The Exorcist*. The three of us leapt up out of the room and ran down the stairs into the kitchen with Millboy following. We slammed the door with the three of us leaning against it so as not to let him in, lest he might try and murder us.

Frankie shouted, 'Randy, Randy.' Then it went quiet and you could just hear him whimpering like a small child woke up from a nightmare.

'Miller,' I said. 'Is that you back again?'

'What happened?' he said.

That night the girls slept together with their arms around each other while me and Millboy lay awake in the next room making hand shadows on the wall. Millboy was headbanging against the bedpost – convinced he was possessed of a spirit. I told him he was mistaken, but it seemed he was past all reason and haunted by what we had done. Other times I would doubt his foolery and consider it a mask worn so as to conceal whatever revenge plot he had brewing in his head.

'What you thinking about?' I said.

'How do you know we ain't transforming into those spirits?' Millboy said.

'What spirits?' I said.

'The ones that Janice Morningstar's always talking about.'

'What makes you think we are?' I said.

'I feel like killing someone.'

'You already did,' I said.

'That was an accident,' Millboy said. 'Next one won't be.'

THE WHITE RIVER MOTELIER

We abandoned the summerhouse and cruised along the Lake Superior coastline, picking up signs from Sudbury and then on to Sault Ste. Marie where a huge iron bridge stood like a giant Meccano set across the river. In the big freeze the rapids had turned to ice and fashioned themselves into silvery waves of crystal glaciers. Disorientated and off track, we pulled into a diner next to a used car lot to bust open the hood of a nearby Ford so we could rip off a battery and syphon off some gasoline with a piece of garden hose cut especially for the occasion. Millboy spat out a mouthful of petrol and lit up a cigarette. Blue and green flames licked around his lips.

'Is this White River?' he said.

'No,' I said. 'It's a service station.'

'I know that,' he said. 'But is it a service station in White River?'

'I don't know.'

'Why not?'

'Because we're lost.'

'How do you know we're lost?'

'Because I don't know where we are.'

'So, we could be in White River?'

'We're not in White River,' I said.

'We could be,' Millboy said. 'We could be anywhere if we're lost.'

Five miles and we picked up signs for the motel. When we arrived, there was a Dixie Lee across the forecourt and we told the girls to wait while we took care of business. The parking lot was empty but a lamp lit up the reception. As I cracked open the car door and stepped out into the cold, a raw-boned man of uncertain age with a platinum backcombed quiff and tinted glasses stood in the doorway.

The White River Motelier beckoned us inside past a collection of teddy bears and lighting equipment. A piano was pushed up against the wall, on top of which were what looked like cut-glass tumblers of urine shining like lamps of varying hues of yellow and orange. There were belt buckles too. Silver rings and costumes hanging from the picture rail. Cameras. Cornhusk dolls with rotting feathers for hair. The motelier took a seat and looked us up and down and said, 'You got the antique? You want a room? Where's the knife? I can do you a room. You two boys sharing? Nice boys. I like that. No rush. We can drink while you check in.'

'We're booksellers,' I said. 'We want some of your dictionaries.'

'Oh, yeah,' he said. 'Who sent you?'

'Romeo,' I said. 'He sent us to make a pickup.'

The White River Motelier took off his tinted glasses to reveal one cool blue eye and a black hole where the other should have been.

'Romeo didn't mention the books. Only the knife. You got the knife?'

Millboy pulled out his fake pistol and said, 'No, but we got this.'

The motelier turned his head slightly so he could focus on the pistol.

'What're you gonna do with that,' he said, 'water the plants?'

Millboy said, 'You've only got one eye. God must have punished you.'

'What do you know about God,' The motelier said. 'You're just a dirty rag that old men use to clean up their mess.'

Millboy put the gun away but shot me a steely look. His lips grew thin.

'We have no money,' he said. 'But we'll take those books anyway. You have mistreated our friends and we intend a reckoning.'

'You're mistaken,' the White River Motelier said. 'I'm just a supplier.'

'Supplier of what?' Millboy said.

'Photographs. Books. Artefacts. Anything you need. I supply stock to people like Romeo and they sell it on, or the other way around. Me and you we're in the same business, we're just working different areas.'

'There ain't nothing about you the same as me,' Millboy said. 'Do not confuse my eye impairment with your own mutated condition. I have known people like you and I don't care much for them.'

The White River Motelier said, 'I deal in curiosities. Objet d'art. I don't involve myself. I like to take pictures. Make films. It's how I remember things.'

The motelier picked up a jar that had what looked like a small onion floating around in some bad milk. 'I am loath to throw it away,' he said. 'I keep it for old time's sake because we have seen a lot of exceptional things together.'

Millboy took the jar and swished it around. 'What kind of things?'

The White River Motelier said, 'The cherry blossom storm of a Japanese spring. The Forbidden City of Beijing and the ping pong girls of Bangkok. They say the memory forgets but the flesh remembers. I sometimes hold that eye in one hand and recollect with the other.'

'You jerk off to a fuckin eye?' Millboy said.

The White River Motelier took back the jar and held it up to the light. You could just about make out the pupil and the dregs of an iris. The White River Motelier shook the jar so that the fibrous strands of whatever holds your eye to your brain swam like worms in the milky solution.

'Do you see that?' he said. 'Do something for me and you'll get the books.'

'Do what?' Millboy said.

'You are not averse to entertaining?'

'What do you mean by entertaining?'

The White River Motelier picked up a camera and turned the lens until it clicked. 'You're the one they call Millboy,' he said. 'I have heard about you. That you live in the towers downtown and sometimes make movies for money. Let me take some pictures. For my collection.'

Millboy's face flashed a mean streak and he reached out and grabbed the motelier by the throat and took the camera and smashed it into the side of the motelier's head and pulled out the film cartridge leaving the black celluloid exposed and unusable. Then he twisted the roll-film around the motelier's neck and pushed him to the ground.

'You're a rotten bastard and I will dig out your good eye with my own fingers and put it somewhere you might enjoy too much if you don't shut your mouth.'

'Aaaw honey,' the supplier said. 'Oh, you sweet thing.'

Outside was frosty and the wind was blowing hard. As we loaded the books into the back of the car, Millboy's hands were bloody and shaking.

There was blood on his boots too.

THE NAMES

Stoney broke and unwashed we crossed the territories and sold some books in Quebec and then back into Ontario, all the while staring out at the endless fields interrupted by new build housing. They seemed to spring up in the most unlikely of places – the gardens still dirt and rubble with towering cranes left for the weekend. Bulldozers and dream billboards.

Make this Place your Home. Canada Calling. It's the new Eldorado.

We drove through December and into January, breaking into empty buildings or sleeping in the car. On the first good day we crossed a bridge and left the Maverick at the side of the road and walked through fields of bright yellow and ate sardines from a can before washing up in the river.

By five it was getting dark, so we made a fire. Spread some blankets on the ground. Cooked some potatoes and opened some beers while Janice played Cat's Cradle in the firelight – her hands like an illusionist as she began to throw shapes – all of us under her spell.

'What sort of name is Morningstar?' Millboy said.

'My father gave it to me,' she said. 'Just like your father gave you yours.'

'My father didn't give me anything,' Millboy said. 'Not even a name.'

'What about your spirit name,' she said. 'Everyone's got one of those.'

'Millboy's the only name I got.'

'Everything in Creation has a spirit name,' Janice said. 'The trees, the animals and plants, all have names. When we receive our spirit name we know who we are. You had a name before you came into this world, and it'll be the same one you take with you when you leave.'

Millboy wanted to know more. 'How do I get a spirit name?'

Janice looped the string around her fingers and magicked up an animal shape. 'In the beginning, He created the animals,' she said. 'And then the rivers and trees. But, He let them choose their own names. You can choose your own name if you like. What kind of name do you want?'

Millboy was interested now. 'Something that'll make people listen to me,' he said. 'No one ever listens to me. They think I am unrefined. It has been mentioned before that I am rude in school. Because of this I was invited to leave the premises by the principal.'

'You seem to have something in common with Coyote,' Janice

Morningstar said. 'He was much misunderstood. He had a twin brother.'

'Coyote had a twin?' Millboy said. 'I had a twin too.'

Janice Morningstar said, 'Coyote tried to stay awake all night so he could be first in line for the naming, but his twin forgot to wake him, so Coyote missed the whole thing. When Coyote woke, he ran to the Chief Spirit and finding no one there, thought he must be the first rather than last. Call me Grizzly Bear, he said. But the Chief, said: You're too late, the Grizzly Bear's gone.

Well alright then, Coyote said. I shall fly like an Eagle. But the Chief said that the Eagle had flown. Well then, Coyote said. Let me be the brightest fish in the river, let me swim with the Salmon. But the Spirit Chief said, The Salmon has swum away. All the names have gone except, Coyote. No one wanted that name. You are the most detested of all animals. But because you are so hated you will have the power to change yourself into any shape you wish. There are monsters on the earth and I give you the power to kill these fiends. I have also given your twin brother the power to help you.'

'So, Coyote never got his name?' Millboy said.

'That's right,' Janice Morningstar said. 'He got stuck with Coyote.'

'And you're stuck with Millboy,' I said.

*

That night we parked outside a school. Climbing over some railings we went around the back and found a secluded spot. The girls stood guard while I hoisted Millboy up on my shoulders and he thumped his fist against the metal window frame with the patience of a habitual housebreaker. The latch jumped and he pulled the window open. It was a small gap but he was smaller and he took off his coat, seeming to dislocate his arms as he squeezed through like a house rat and dropped down, finding the fire exit and opening the door with a flourish, as if he were a disappearing act come back to take a bow from the audience.

We ran through the corridors, trying the handles. All the classrooms and offices were locked, so we kicked open some of the doors and rooted around until we found a cashbox in an administrative office. We smashed that open and took the money. Then we broke into the chapel and stole some holy water. Millboy had stomach pains and said holy water was the best cure and then went at it like a baby sucking on a tit before filling up the pistol and baptising us in the name of Randy Miller.

'I'm gonna wash away all your sins,' he said. 'Take the pain away.'

In the canteen we fired up the industrial cookers. Giant cans of processed meat, tinned vegetables and pasta. We ate until we were sick and threw cooked spaghetti around so that it stuck to the walls and hung from the ceiling. In the main hall we found boxes of clothes and props strewn about. It looked like they were putting on a production of *A Christmas Carol* or something of that nature. We dressed up in the stage clothes, parading around the room like dandies and dudes. Frankie wore a blue velvet morning jacket with a cardboard top hat and carried a cane, while Millboy came out with makeup on his face wearing a brightly coloured dress gathered up and worn over another skirt. He topped off the whole get-up with a straw hat, trimmed with plastic cherries and yellow ribbons.

'How do I look?' he said.

'Like a tart,' I said.

'I feel immortal,' he said. 'Like a whole person.'

'Maybe your twin was a girl?' I said.

'It's not beyond the realms of possibility,' he said. 'Feels like it's downtown Halloween, and I'm on parade.'

Millboy started dancing with Frankie while Janice Morningstar passed around a joint. We got stoned on a bottle of wine and slept wrapped up in the long curtains torn down from the back of the stage. Frankie and Millboy curled around each other while Janice lay next to me. Her scent like a river running through a forest. Her hands finding mine, and as our fingers entwined, I felt her press up against me as she moved one of her arms around my waist and unzipped my fly and I came in her fist.

The next morning Frankie wasn't speaking to us. Back on the road Millboy was stood up driving. His face almost touching the windshield. Tiger riding shotgun. The whole atmosphere undercut with an air of misery. I was in the back with Frankie on one side and Janice on the other. An old blanket covered the three of us, and with no back window it was like driving through a whirlwind.

Janice Morningstar nestled her head next to mine. Her breath hot and her lips whispering something sweet into my neck. Before long, her hands moved into my lap and she put her head under the blanket.

I leaned back and closed my eyes.

I'm not sure how long I slumbered, but when Millboy slowed to take a corner, Frankie opened the door, falling out and rolling across the grit before getting up and walking along the roadside like a person who didn't care much about anything.

Millboy told Frankie to get back in the car, but she just sat down and sprawled over the ground like someone who'd just crawled out of the wreckage.

I didn't feel good about the business with Janice, but it was just one of them things that happen when you're young or maybe no good.

'C'mon, Frankie,' I said. 'What's the matter with you? It's not such a big deal.'

'You don't take care of me, Turner,' Frankie said. 'I'm finished with you. Maybe you should go back to wherever you came from.'

Millboy stared me down. 'If it wasn't for you we'd have been back in Toronto by now,' he said. 'Everything would have been peachy creamo instead of fucked up, which is what it is.'

'You hid the money,' I said. 'That's how it all started.'

'Yeah, well you found it,' Millboy said.

'And you spent it,' I said.

'Why don't you fuck off,' Millboy said.

'C'mon, Millboy.'

'You fuck off.'

'All right, then.'

'You fuck off.'

Millboy wore a dress but I lashed out anyway and caught him on the side of the head and he threw a punch but it went wide. That made Frankie stand up and smack me so hard that my ear started bleeding again.

'Leave him alone,' she said. 'We all spent that money.'

'It's always been you two,' I said. 'You and him.'

We drove on in silence – past a giant carved rock face; waterways and a rainforest; an old man was selling white quartz arrowheads and pottery fragments at the side of the road. We stopped to take a look. Janice Morningstar said she was going to spend some time with relatives up North and would hitch a ride.

'I have brought some trouble to you,' she said. 'It's time for me to leave.'

'Everybody's quitting,' Millboy said. 'Fuckum's what I say.'

The last of the melting snow was heaped at the side of the road. Dirty and salted and clearing a path for the traffic that now gathered and streamed out from the provinces and back towards the city calling us home.

WELCOME STRANGER

The sun sat small and yellow in a pale blue sky that looked like someone had taken a child's crayon and drawn a pink line across it. We'd been sleeping in the car and washing at truck stops and stealing food or going hungry most of the time. It was still early and we had the whole day ahead of us when we stopped for breakfast.

No cars were parked and a sign read *Welcome Stranger*.

Millboy played the toe of his shoe into a dead bird – its skull hollowed out and one wing flapping optimistically in the breeze. Frankie pushed the replica pistol inside her shirt and chewed on her fingernails.

'I don't want to go back to my old ways,' she said. 'First thing I'm going to do when we get home, is take a shower and sleep for a week. Then I'm going to fill in that form for college.'

We entered the store. A woman with a hatchet head appeared and started following us around. Me and Millboy split into different aisles and lifted goods while Frankie distracted the woman by paying for some cigarettes and juice with what little money we had left.

'That's not enough,' Hatchet Head said.

'That's the exact right amount,' Frankie said. 'You ain't looking hard enough.'

You could see the hard outline of the pistol packed tight under Frankie's shirt. Hatchet Head picked up the money but kept a beady eye on Frankie's tit.

Didn't seem much like a *Welcome Stranger* to me.

Outside was cold in the way it is early in the day. We got back in the Maverick and breakfasted on stolen grape juice and potato chips with the heater blowing its bad breath around. I reckoned we were maybe two or three hours from the city and turned on the car radio.

Blondie singing 'Union City Blues'.

Millboy found a small piece of something he reckoned was dope but could have been dried cat shit and he rolled that into a joint. Frankie crashed on the backseat with Tiger and I shifted the gear stick into drive, and we headed for the TransCanada Highway at the legal speed limit of 40mph.

Couldn't have been more than five minutes until I heard the whining of the Ontario State Police coming right up behind with a red-light flashing.

I slowed down hoping the car would overtake but it just pulled back.

In the rear view I could see the cop.

All buzzcut and shades – committed to a course of action.

Millboy had climbed over the seats and was now laid out in the back with his feet stuck out the window and his head in Frankie's lap reading the comic pages from a newspaper he'd just stolen.

'Sit up,' I said. 'Act normal.'

Millboy swung his feet around and poked his head out the back window.

'Stop staring,' I said. 'You're just making it worse.'

Frankie said, 'Perhaps the cop doesn't like the message we're sending?'

'What message?' I said.

'Telling him everyone thinks he's an asshole except for Jesus Christ.'

'Amen,' Millboy said.

I made some turns and slowed but the police kept following. I prayed that a simple handing over of the replica pistol and an explanation would be enough and pulled the Maverick over onto the grassy verge. I cut the engine and told everyone to stay in the car and asked Frankie for the pistol.

The police pulled up behind with the red-light still flashing in the sunlight.

*

Sometimes the smallest thing will happen and it can change your life forever. Right then it felt like the shell of an egg had broken and a sick thing had crawled out and died right inside of me.

*

Millboy was brawling with Frankie. I was trying to intervene. From where the cop was parked it must have looked like we were all fighting. I grabbed Millboy by the shirt collar and yelled in his face telling him to stay in the car, but he started climbing back over the seat, waving that fake pistol around and practically foaming at the mouth as he yelled back at me.

'How come you get to make all the rules, Turner? I'm sick of your shit and telling everyone what to do. I know what's good for me and I'm doing it.'

Millboy fell out the Maverick, picking himself back up before ambling across the road as if everything was just fine. The Ontario State Police dropped for cover behind his driver's door. The wind was so low that you could hear the sound of snow crackling in the cold sun. Millboy still in semi drag now standing on the hard shoulder with his hands held high.

His shadow stretched out in front of him like a giant in the sun. 'It's nothing,' he shouted.

Then Millboy opened his hand to show the cop what nothing looked like and the sound of a gunshot ricocheted across the open fields, and I saw Randy Miller drop like a heap of rags thrown on the ground with his brains splashing red on the cold icy verge as his gold scalp fell softly to the side.

Frankie ran over and picked up what must have been a piece of his head and tried to reattach it like you might a broken piece of china to a bowl. Apart from the top of his head missing he looked all right, but whatever it was makes you alive was gone.

The cop took off his shades. He had a smattering of freckles and his eyes were the colour of sand. He didn't seem much older than us and had the name BRIAN stitched to his shirt. 'From where I was, looked like a real gun,' he said. 'If the kid had stayed in the car, he would have been all right but now I've got to deal with all this and it's the first time I've been out on my own.'

Brian's lip started to tremble and he sniffled the last sentence as if it was him that'd been shot and not Millboy.

'What're you crying for?' Frankie said. 'You didn't even know him?'

The static on Brian's radio broke and a mess of voices came over the shortwave. Before too long you could see the dust rising up over the hill. The sirens moaned and the engines cut through the quiet of the morning changing the day into something that was not there before. Millboy's head now rested in a pool of blood and there were bugs on his face. I brushed them off.

'You didn't have to do that,' I said.

Brian restored himself to the full height of an Ontario state police officer and put his radio away. 'I know who you are,' he said. 'You're those Toronto kids. The ones causing all that trouble. The whole force's been out looking for you.'

'Go to hell,' Frankie said.

PART THREE

Toronto

AT THE TREATMENT CENTRE

After what happened they said I was all right but that Frankie needed treatment. It was decided that we could not meet and an order was passed. I asked Ray about Frankie and he said she'd been sick and made out that it might be in the head rather than the body. They took me to a place out in Etobicoke and kept me in for checks and asked questions about whether or not I thought it was normal to steal cars and run around having masturbation fantasies about my mother.

They asked me about my friends and I said I only had two and one of them was dead and I wasn't allowed to see the other.

They asked me about school and why I stopped going and I told em about the business with the name and they wrote something down in their book about that before asking me if I had mastur-bation fantasies about Mr. Carpenter and I said no and took great offence, as I expect would Mr. Carpenter.

They asked me about my memory and I feigned not to remember much as my sleeping patterns were all messed up on account of the emotional trauma and they wrote something down in their book again.

They asked me if I felt sad, so I just started crying and that wasn't even pretending.

Did I have a problem with aggression?

I didn't think so, but they noted the tone of my reply and wrote that down too. At one point there were three of them all with clip-boards and a tape machine whirring away.

They asked about substance abuse and I said not lately but on occasion and in the past. They searched my arms for track marks but there were none.

They asked me if I was paranoid or suspicious and I said I wasn't up until that point, but that all the questions were making me so, and one of em looked at the other and they wrote something down in their book again.

They understood that the family breakup and subsequent relo-cation was an emotional upset but that was no excuse for what happened, and I had to agree that point.

They asked me about my relationship with Randy Miller and Frankie Lee. They made out Millboy was a warped individual. Damaged was the word they used. Did I know about his home life and what he did to make money at bus stations and in the public lavatories downtown? That he was an errand boy for the rub n tugs. That he had been known to the authorities.

They said the situation with Frances Lee was unsustainable, like it was limited by time or something else that I was too young to understand.

They'd spoken to Mr. Carpenter. They'd spoken to Farley and Hatchet Head. For all I knew, they'd spoken to the Elastic Man. From what I could gather Quohog still swam at the bottom of the lake. Nobody mentioned the White River Motelier and nobody mentioned the Devil's Children or even Romeo. They just seemed hung up on us threatening the shopkeeper with a water pistol. I told em we were no thrill-kill cult and that we were just ordinary dictionary salesmen on a delivery job gone wrong.

They put me in a room and watched me through glass. They said I was allowed to go home but would have to report back at some point in the near future at a date they would decide on.

I was not considered a risk.

FRANKIE LEE

Each night I would hold Frankie's shirt to my face and breathe in her scent – the trace of woodfire: Tiger. I kept the Polaroid in a tobacco tin, the one signed with a fingernail X – the background a blur and Frankie's face washed out against the flash. Other days I went over to Regent Park and wandered through the courtyards. I didn't expect her to care, I just wanted her to know.

One Sunday I sat all day on a wall reading a paperback about a group of friends who get lost up river. Just when I was at the part when one of them dreams of a dead man's hand rising from the lake, I heard a voice.

'What are you doing around here? We're not supposed to meet.'

Frankie looked older, her hair darker. She had on a yellow ski jacket and a light blue silk neck scarf. She was eating an apple and looked like a college student. I put the book back in my pocket and said, 'I just wanted to see you.'

We took a walk to Union Station and rode a streetcar to Cherry Beach. We found a café and shared a Coke and cheeseburger. Frankie took out some picture cards and arranged them on the table and said she dreamed about her father every night. He appeared as the Duke and would climb up on to a high bed and she would massage his blubber until there was nothing left but a carcass of skin and bones heaped up on the floor.

'That's just the way of dreams,' I said. 'Everything gets all mixed up. Even the faces of people you know.'

'I didn't know my father,' she said.

'And you don't know the Duke, either,' I said.

'But it's like the Duke made those pictures and put them in my head,' she said. 'Like it wasn't enough what they done. They have to own my dreams too.'

Frankie opened her jacket and her shirt was damp in patches, and in my ignorance, I didn't understand what she was showing me or even trying to say.

'What is that?' I said.

'That is what happens when you're going to have a baby,' she said. 'That's the milk coming out. I'm supposed to wear pads but I keep forgetting.'

'You're going to have a baby?'

'That's what they tell me.'

'When?'

'I don't know. They're trying to work it out. That's why I can't see you.'

Part of me was excited and another part confused and if I admit, disbelieving of the whole situation, and that's when I said the stupidest thing I ever said to anyone in my whole life so far.

'Is it mine?'

Frankie got up and headed for the door.

'I hate you, Turner,' she said. 'Why don't you just leave me alone.'

I read somewhere that if you want to know what someone is thinking you just have to arrange your face into their expression and those thoughts will come naturally into your head.

This is what I did and I did not like those thoughts.

EXHIBITION PLACE

As part of my rehabilitation I had to get a job. Each morning Ray would drop me off at the steel plant and I'd set to work in an industrial unit with a gas torch, bending steel rods for twenty dollars a day. I kept to myself and ate my lunch well away from the others. At the end of every week I collected my wages and put some money aside. I could feel myself getting stronger. At that time my dreams were often wild – a knife like a ragged giant tooth in my hand; a horned bird with red wings coming at me. Overcome with an emotion I could not understand, I was reminded of what Janice Morningstar said.

What is it you're so afraid of that you start to think the only way to stop the horror is to destroy the thing that's making you afraid?

I could've grabbed that pistol and thrown it out the window, or put my foot down and given the police something to chase. I could have got out the car and dragged Millboy back inside.

For a long time afterward, I couldn't sleep nights and used to stand with the palms of my hands flat on the bedroom wall thinking about what happened. It felt like if I'd lifted my hands, the whole world would've come tumbling down.

Sometimes I'd stay there all night, holding that wall up.

In that time Millboy came to me. We sat like puppets on a stage with our backs against the wall looking straight into an empty dancehall, batting away flaming marbles of fire that spun like tiny planets, softly burning before turning to ash.

I wish I'd never done it, Turner. I should've stayed in the car. I made a mistake. Who would have thought that fat cop would have been such a good shot? Maybe he got lucky. Everyone can get lucky once and unlucky too. Must have been my unlucky day. It's lonely here. I got no one to hang with.

During these dreams I'd awake with night sweats feeling like I'd been sent a message of some kind, but didn't know what it meant or what to do about it.

I went to see Gramps and he told me Millboy was a fantasist and that the mother was still alive and remarried to someone else on the other side of town. There was no room for Millboy, what with all the other kids she had, so Gramps took him in. It was either that or be taken into social care. There was never any twin and Gramps didn't know nothing about Elvis, except he was a fat slob who couldn't sing.

Gramps gave me a blue shirt that belonged to Millboy and said I could take anything else I wanted, but there was nothing else, so I went outside and pulled on that blue shirt as if it might show me the way or at least give me some comfort. Then I took a ride to Exhibition Place and jumped a barrier, stooping under some ropes and picking up a hard hat to make out I was inspecting the equipment.

Up close you could see the rock walls were fake and the fibreglass, now smashed through with gaping holes, revealed twisted steel and marbled paint. The *Guess my Weight* lady may have vanished but the Elastic Man was still there. Tall and slender and smoking a cigar. The blue fug that came out of his lungs hung in a swell above his head. The skin covering his bony hands like cracked leather in the sun. He gave me the side-eye and started walking.

I followed the Elastic Man and he stopped to turn and look as if trying to figure out who I was or remember what con he'd pulled. I grabbed him by the neck and stretched out the scaly membrane until he looked like a frilled lizard.

'Remember me?' I said.

'Leave me alone,' he said.

I thought it might feel good to smash him in the face, but before I could make my mind up, two hundred and fifty pounds of carney came out of nowhere and knocked me down. When I got back up the carney was waving an iron tent stake at me. 'Go back to town,' he yelled. 'Don't come around here no more, unless you want to lose your teeth.'

I backed off and ran until I got heartburn, then took the subway to Regent Park where Kathy Lee answered the door stone-faced and high on pills.

'She's not here.'

'I know she's here Kathy Lee. I just saw her sneaking around behind you.'

'She doesn't want to speak to you, Turner. Just go.'

I shouted out Frankie's name, but some guy standing behind Kathy Lee was glaring over her shoulder. I pushed the door and tried to step in but he filled the frame, making it clear he was going to enjoy breaking me apart.

'Try it,' he said.

Kathy Lee came back to the door with a grocery bag full of books and tapes. 'Take these,' she said, 'Frankie don't need em. She got that place in college and you're not going to stop her. I'll phone Ray if I have to – what you did to her.'

My face burned with shame. I took the bag and jumped the stairs one flight at a time. The soles of my feet stinging as they slapped down hard on the surface of the tiles. I ran through the courtyards of Regent Park and leaped over the low walls, tearing up the flowerbed.

Someone yelled from a window, and I yelled back.

Out into the streets and through the trade lanes. Between the cars and trucks and then through Old Town and the tall buildings where I ditched the bag in a skip and sat on a bench. And that's when I saw his name spray-painted on the wall in big red letters like a STOP sign.

There were some derelicts drinking and playfighting. I waited until they had left and then squeezed beneath a bent-up metal door and found myself in the concrete stairwell of a fire escape where I shouted out his name before hearing it come back like some signal from another world.

His voice in my head on a loop.

All roads lead to the same place. Don't matter which one you choose. You'll find out when you get to the top that there's nowhere else to go.

I began to climb the stairs. The city rose up like a stone forest. Down below the people wandered the walkways. Street after street of railway lines and ravines that carved up the town into a grid – cities within cities.

C'mon, Turner. You can do it.

A tightness of hard knots flared in my guts. I wanted to reach down my throat or take a knife to my stomach and rip them out. I wanted to fill my ears with dirt and stop the voice.

You should've made me stay in the car, Turner. You should've kept your hands to yourself. If it wasn't for you everything would be peachy creamo. It was you that killed Quohog and it was you that got me shot and that's why Frankie's leaving. Because you're no good. It's not your fault. There's just something in you that's bad. You were born that way. Everybody knows. Ray knows, your mother too. Why do you think she left? You even saw it yourself when you looked in the mirror? You're broken and can't be fixed. That's how it is with some people and there's nothing that can be done about it.

When I got to the top there was a small ladder welded to the wall that led to a chamber and above that a circular hole that was boarded over. I reached up and pushed the panel and it lifted. I pulled myself into a space that was the size of a small room or church belfry.

Inside was a sleeping bag next to a camping stove. A tiny radio was jammed on the sill. I opened a safety hatch and crawled through a small window onto a ledge and looked down at the street far below. The urge to close my eyes and lean into that open space, almost overwhelming.

C'mon, Turner. There's nothing to it.

Down below the people were small and the lights just a haze of colour. I thought about Millboy and what I had done to Frankie. My head felt like it was full of crows and my thoughts were mixed-up and as I considered all the actions that had led me to this place, I soon came to hating the whole world and everything in it.

ROMEO SILVA

The building was a redbrick square at the corner of Queen Street East and Broadview Avenue. Romeo's English Jag was parked outside. A string of bulbs hung across the doorway – hot pink and purple. Some white silhouettes of long-legged women spinning around a pole were stuck on blacked-out windows. There was a sick-faced man in a kiosk taking money and crossing the backs of hands with a marker pen. He picked some pox off of his face and chewed on it so you could see the green roots of his yellow teeth. Then he spat out a scab and said, 'You got any I.D?'

'I need to see Romeo,' I said. 'I got something for him.'

He gave me a creepy smile. 'I bet you do,' he said.

The club had a fake Mediterranean theme constructed out of

chicken wire and papier-mâché stalactites that hung down from the ceiling and occasionally fell or were ripped off and used as weapons.

It was mid-afternoon and full of suits and construction workers. The stink of sweat mixed with cigarettes and alcohol. There were gas pipes and wires hanging down and I recognized the man from Kathy Lee's apartment standing guard just in case someone tried to touch the girls.

I took a plastic cup of beer and watched the show from behind a column. As the lunch hour rolled on the men got wilder, meaner, shouting out and throwing dollar bills that were now littering the platform or pushed into the elastic at the side of the girls' pants. There was a tableful of cheese spread sandwiches and I ate one, stuffed another in my pocket, and then watched as Kathy Lee swung her jugs around with the silver tassels spinning to the music that was feeding back through the speakers.

'Hot Child in the City'.

Under the harsh light, Kathy Lee's face was a greasy mask and her ass was round and hard like a basketball. I watched for a while and then followed Romeo into the washroom and waited. The toilet stunk of weed and the floor trembled with an overflow that soaked the hem of my jeans and seeped through the holes in my pumps. Romeo belched and broke wind, then zipped up his fly and combed his hair with his fingers before telling me to follow him back into the club. As we pushed through the crowd the girls danced in a circle: their bodies oiled – the music loud. On the ceiling: Kathy Lee reflected and broken up in the mirrorball.

Romeo Silva walked me to the exit but took a sharp right, and pushed me up some stairs and kept pushing and then kicked open the fire door.

Up on the roof you could see blocks of grey stone stretched out toward lakeshore amid half-built condos. The concrete pod of the CN Tower dominated the horizon. White jet trails crisscrossed a clear blue sky. Romeo stood holding a newspaper with a headline that read:

Motorcyclist Missing

'The Devil's Children want me dead,' he said. 'They want me dead. Do you hear me? I've been getting death threats because of you pricks. Because you failed to do one simple job. Where's the antique you were supposed to pick up? Where's my money? And by the way, what happened to Quohog?'

'It went wrong,' I said. 'Quohog pulled a knife on Millboy. They started to fight. It was an accident.'

'I should have known that shithead would screw it up. A boy like that can only go both ways. Frankie, too. Any idea who the father is? Could be anyone, I heard. Even me.'

A ball of poison formed in my gut and I swallowed hard and brought up some mucus and spat right in his face. The sputum dangled off his cheek in a kaleidoscopic slime ball. He gave some-one the nod and I went down. When I came around the world was the wrong way up and my wrists were tied behind my back. The silvery blue of the lake now the sky as my head smashed against the steel rungs of a ladder.

When I was turned upright I found myself above a large cistern used to collect rain water. The top of the cistern was missing and I was hung over the side. The serrated edge dug into the top of my thighs and cut through my jeans. Below me a shallow slop of just a few inches and the fur and bones of something dead and the rotting husks of a thousand bugs.

They bounced me into the sludge and left me there. I held my breath for as long as I could but started to choke. They swung me around by my legs and dropped me again. As I tumbled into the darkness a shock of blue lightning exploded behind my eyes and I started to panic.

Romeo kept shouting. 'Where's Quohog? Where's the knife?'

I knew the terrain as a place where pale horses stood at the gate. A large oak where the road turned. The wood frame house next to the lake at the bottom of a valley. I told him as much and then heard the clang of the metal cover being dragged back over and felt the burn of slurry as it dribbled out of my nose.

An intense sense of claustrophobia overwhelmed me and I let go.

*

Caught in the crossfire of my parents fighting I would sometimes hideaway in the garden. There was a bush behind a small stone wall. A leafy doorway where the border closed behind so that it grew dark. I would push myself as far back as I could and curl up into a ball and imagine a small white space that turned into a large white space. It would get so that you couldn't tell where the walls stood or whether there was a floor or ceiling anymore – and there you were. Suspended in the middle of a perfectly translucent cube.

It was my special place of absolute knowledge.

*

My mother had always wanted to be an actress, but a job at a TV rental store was as close to working in television as she got. At home she would tap dance around the kitchen singing songs from the musicals. Sometimes she would just sit in a room on her own. For a while Ray was an insurance salesman. He sold used cars. Once he had the idea of cat boxes: fur lined mini plywood cat-caves that he had made up at the local carpentry workshop. The house was filled with so many cat-caves that you could hardly open the door. We waited for the orders but nothing rolled in. Not even tumbleweed. Then it was camping supplies. On the Eve of New Year, they split. While the neighbours stood in a circle outside and sang drunkenly the promise of what the future might bring, my mother locked herself in a room. In that way I was like her. I had been to that place and knew there was nothing to fear.

Solitude could be a sanctuary.

Just before she left for good, I caught her sat on the edge of the bed with a suitcase half-packed and an empty bottle of brandy. Her belly flab hung over the top of her slacks and her face a mess of makeup. She opened her arms and hugged me so tight I nearly stopped breathing.

Ah, Turner. You know I love you, don't you?

*

I'm not sure how long I hung upside down, but I managed to work off the flex and pull myself the right way up so that I was standing in the tank. The cheese snack was still in my pocket so I ate that and punched the cover off and climbed out into the daylight. My fingernails bloody. The wind whistling through the rooftop wires. The fire exit was locked and there didn't seem to be anyway down except the long way. On the other side of the roof,

133

there was some dead space and a thick cable connected one build to a redbrick across the street with a drop down to a flat roof of perhaps fifty feet. I looped my belt around the cable and twisted my legs around to take the weight before shimmying across, but then stopped halfway. Working at the factory may have made my arms stronger, my hands tougher, but all I had to do was touch an exposed line and I'd be Kentucky Fried, hanging like a bird on a wire.

I started again and felt the cable slacken, spark and then snap.

I put my feet out and broke the fall and tumbled onto a lower rooftop. I kicked open a door and ran down a stairwell straight onto Broadview Avenue. From there I took a long walk up to Yonge and then into the Eaton and tried my best to clean up in the restroom before going out into the street where I panhandled for fifteen minutes and then found shelter in a grindhouse theatre where I fell asleep and woke to find some smoky old fruit fondling my balls.

THE NEON D

Maybe Quohog was nothing now but bones scattered across the bottom of the lake or a bad dream that would follow us around the rest of our lives. Maybe I'd become that hollow thing Janice Morningstar was always talking about. I felt like a cloud that might burst or even a storm. I was nauseous and swallowing bugs. The bugs crawled into my ears and laid eggs in my brain. I wandered the streets till it got dark and kept walking through a long night. Past the head shops and peep shows, the record stores and street hustlers. Cinema 2000: *The Big Snatch*. Yonge Street is Fun Street. The glitzy emporiums of a neon slum.

At a crossroads downtown, I watched the tall towers light up like cathedrals and closed my eyes and prayed. But it seemed like nothing could save me, and the only way I could leave the past behind was to go back there, so I took a subway to York Mills and hitched a ride in a food truck before passing out.

*

By the time we reached the Neon D it was noon. The diner was half-full with travellers and truckers. Mostly men. The unwed, the separated and divorced. Over in the corner the Wurlitzer was playing 'Only the Lonely' as an overworked busboy cleared the tables. I thought I could smell his armpits but it might have been the food. I ordered an omelette and French fries and took my rightful place among the lonely.

On the far side of the café Janice Morningstar was serving coffee. Her hair was longer and tied back. She wore a beaded choker and a bright red cap. When she saw me, she walked over and rubbed her eyes with her fist.

'I have to work, Turner. I can't afford to lose this job. What are you doing here, anyhow?'

'I'm going back,' I said.

Janice Morningstar took off her smock and asked the busboy to cover for her and we went outside. There was a greasy stain on the parking lot where Quohog's brains had bled out. We stood under the Neon D and smoked. Janice Morningstar rubbed her eyes again and looked at the shirt I was wearing and ran her fingers across the buttons.

'How's Frankie?' she said.

'I don't know,' I said. 'She isn't talking to me. You heard what happened to Miller, anyway?'

'Millboy got himself killed and now you will,' she said. 'The Duke's been in asking questions. They took Quohog's motorcycle. They're looking for Romeo. They think he knows where Quohog is. That's why you should stay away. They think Romeo's got the dagger. I didn't say anything that might change their mind.'

'The dagger,' I said. 'Why is it so important?'

'It's not just a dagger,' she said. 'And it's not the money. All things have a power. Even that shirt you're wearing. They think the knife has a kind of magic. That's why they want it. They see it as a talisman that will protect them from their enemies. But the opposite is true. You can't just take things that don't belong to you.'

Janice Morningstar told me to take Millboy's shirt off and burn it and never say his name again. She told me I had to let him go.

'Stay away from the summerhouse,' she said. 'Go home, Turner.'

THE SUMMERHOUSE

The summerhouse looked different with the snow gone. Purple buds flowered and ducks hugged the edge of a lake thick with root leaves and plants that twisted up out of the slime and then dropped back down again. The surface of the lake was humming with bugs and alive with islands of bright green algae. When you got up close you could see silvery insects skating across the surface like tiny gods. Across the way the horses watched. Their new coats shining in the fading light that now spread out across the hills producing a pinkish glow that coloured the whole landscape.

The door to the house was wide open. Inside the creak and groan of the floorboards. There was bird mess and what looked like coyote scat and even horsehair from the Chesterfield strewn around.

Jim Reeves was still on the stereo player. I placed the needle on the record and walked through the house pulling out desk drawers and searching the back of picture frames.

All the time, Jim Reeves was singing his heart out.

Knock and the door will open, seek and you will find.

I went upstairs into the bedroom. There was blood on the sheets. Blood on the walls. The ceramic frog lay broken in half on the floor. An empty wine bottle stuck through a hole in the door and a used tampon was hanging from a nail.

The Nunleys would not be best pleased.

In the kitchen, Janice Morningstar's sketch of the summerhouse remained, and next to it, the drawing of a jagged blade. I went outside and intoxicated by the sweet, sharp scent, walked up through the spruce and pine until I found myself back at Millboy's hut. The door stuck fast and covered in ivy. The winter had left the rotting roof caved in from heavy snow. I climbed up a fallen tree and crawled in through a hole.

When I dropped down I nearly went through the floor. As I removed my leg from the smashed wood, I found myself looking at something wrapped in newspaper and tied up with string. Small shells of coral and ivory and bright beads of turquoise shaped in patterns of dancing animal men were stitched into the leather.

The dagger was bone handled and must have been ten inches long. I took it out and ran my fingers down the edge of the blade and held the tip to my throat and felt the point press into my Adam's apple, but nothing came of it. Instead I kicked open the door of the hut and stepped outside. A coyote loped away into the woods. I followed it down to the sound of car wheels breaking on grit and watched as an English Jag parked on the dirt patch outside the backdoor of the summerhouse.

As the car door swung open, Romeo stepped out and I felt the hate rise up in my throat, my hand gripping that knife like it had been placed there by fate asking me to deliver a message from another world.

From the cover of the trees I watched as Romeo went inside the summerhouse and came back with a long metal pole and makeshift net. He took a torch from the English Jag and climbed into the boat and rowed out into the middle of the lake and stood astride the boat gently rocking. Then he took the pole and started fishing around – pushing under the surface and bringing up clumps of dark green weeds before throwing them back again. When he got up close to where the tall grass sprang from the surface, he took a torch and got down on his hands and knees, shining the light directly on top of the lake; only this time he took the pole like he was trying to thread a giant needle or not startle something that was alive and might swim away.

They say dusk is the best time to go fishing. Something to do with the way those freaks crawl out of their holes looking to feed once the sun has set.

As Romeo gazed down, his face mirrored the light reflected in the water and his expression changed considerably. Maybe he could see the boat or the outline of a boat. Whatever it was made him stand up in anticipation and raise high that metal pole, but as he did, Quohog came up with his arms outstretched like some effigy from the deep, his charred remains now unrecognisable – his hands like stumps and his genitals eaten away so that there was a hole the size of your fist in his lower torso. Some crabs clung to his face and his one arm was bent all wrong but still held together by the biker jacket.

Romeo held onto that metal rod like he was doing battle with some monster from the deep. The green water drained from the foul body back into the lake. For a moment I thought Romeo might throw what was left of Quohog back, but instead he hauled the carcass into the boat where it offset the balance and tilted the craft, bringing the corpse down so that he fell all snarled up in that awful muck and mess and back into the water with Quohog wrapped around his neck.

I stood around waiting and hoping Romeo might drown, but somehow, he managed to thrash his way back to the boat where he hung on and kicked his legs until he got to the lakeside where he pulled himself and what was left of Quohog back out onto the grass. And as he lay there, gasping and puking up black water, I thought about stabbing him to death. I thought about fetching the kerosene from the woodshed. Instead I tossed Romeo's car keys into the lake and hitched a ride back into town with a passing truck.

The driver handed me a bottle of beer and offered me a cigarette and said he was glad of the company. Loretta Lynn on the radio. Hot smoke in my lungs. The knife in my boot. The Devil's Children roaring past in the direction of the summerhouse.

Looking like they meant business.

STRAY DOGS

After what happened I caught a bug that put me in bed for three weeks. I must have lost twenty pounds because my jeans kept falling down and my cheeks grew hollow and pale. For a while I didn't shave or shower, but just laid in my own stink, hallucinating and mostly dreaming on Frankie. By the time I'd sweated out the fever and recovered from my lunacy, it was early spring.

Outside there were riots going on. The cops were cleaning up the city. Some monsters had murdered an errand boy – a child of the streets. An innocent flowerchild just trying to earn a buck. He'd been lured and gang raped and drowned in a sink by a group of men who left him out on the rooftops for the birds to peck at. People wanted blood. Thousands marched. There was moral panic. Innocents got blamed. Drag queens – the gay community got targeted.

I kept my own counsel and bought the newspapers everyday expecting to read something about Romeo and the poisoned lake but did not. Instead, a story about a floater in Lake Ontario who had been identified by his teeth. On the second page, a story about hungry coyotes, plaguing the city and eating cats and scaring the citizens.

God's own dog.

*

It seems the Douchebag was just a pack of coyotes from the edge of town. The city sprawl had encroached on their hunting ground so they came looking for food. The coyotes would drag the cats back to their den under the storm drain and pile up a stack of rotten heads and tails. When a dog walker came across the corpses, he called the cops.

Sometimes things are just straightforward like that.

There was no voodoo. No Douchebag. And no fat masturbator.

The Toronto authorities class coyotes as vermin. Unwanted scavengers that prey on the city. Stray dogs that move in the shadows. If you're lucky enough to see one out on the streets at night, take a look. As still as a figure in a picture book.

Yellow eyes burning like liquid gold in the darkness.

*

Sometimes I would visit Millboy's tower and make it my hideaway. Curl up into a tight ball until the world seemed bearable again. I felt guilty about everything and one night drank too much and passed out. When I awoke I had a fierce hunger and my mouth was so dry I couldn't speak. There was a brass tap on the wall and I drank the metallic tasting water until my stomach swelled and then drank some more and waited a while and thought I might puke but just pissed a fuzzy dark brown into a bucket. Then drank some more and pissed a clear yellow before laying down and slumbering for what seemed like an hour but might have been an entire day for all I know.

When I awoke it was to an almighty racket in the space directly below. I thought it might be those derelicts from before, so picked up the gas stove and stood back, waiting to whac-a-mole, but when the panel moved away I saw it was Frankie Lee. I pulled her up and she put her arms around me as if it was the last time she was ever going to hold me.

'I had a baby,' she said. 'They took him away but I got to nurse him for a short while. He was a beautiful thing. As perfect as any angel. They said I was too far gone for a termination. They put me in a maternity home with some other girls. We had to say our prayers every night and ask for forgiveness and the newborns were taken for the sake of their own health and welfare. He's all right now and with a family someplace in north Ontario. I wrote his name on my arm with a pin.'

Frankie pushed up the sleeve of her jacket to show me an inky scrawl enclosed within a heart shaped homemade tattoo. I traced the letters with my finger. 'Jim Reeves,' I said. 'Is there a photograph?'

'They wouldn't let me have one,' she said. 'But I took a picture in my head. You should see him, Turner. His face all soft and velvety. Like a small animal. All wrapped up in a blanket. He looks just like you but fatter. Even has that frown that makes you look mean all the time.'

In the quiet of that space above the city, we held on to each other and listened to the sounds of the street as they played shrill and soft like a radio turned down. Stargazing – I watched the taillight from an airplane as it moved across Frankie's body. Her hair was damp and smelled of apples. She curled into me and we slumbered.

The city like a dream.

When I awoke, Frankie was kissing me, pulling off her clothes and tugging at mine. Her breath sour and lips dry. Outside the chattering of the birds was like a mad rush and as the chamber filled with light I felt the warmth of the sun wash over me and under me as one by one the knots came undone in my stomach and then there was no use for a name or even words, and I closed my eyes and slept for a good while after that.

THE COLLEGIATE INSTITUTE

I arrived at the Collegiate Institute and walked around the perimeter of the school and stood under a tree and smoked. A flock of birds shapeshifted in a dull spring sky. I kicked through the leaves, watching the janitor watching me. We circled each other from a distance until he got distracted by some students coming out at the sound of the bell – young men and women, athletic and wholesome with a confidence I could not relate to and was resentful of. They seemed to know where they were going in a world that was made just for them.

*

Time passed and tired of waiting I went in through the swing doors and walked the empty corridors. The hum of electricity as fluorescent tubes flickered overhead. The sound of my footsteps echoing through the building. I had a feeling Carpenter might know something about the knife as he would often talk about tribal customs and ancient crafts and sometimes offer field trips out to the country. Some lockers were open, so I slammed one shut with the palm of my hand and Carpenter opened his office door and looked around until he saw me.

'Is that you, John?'

I didn't correct him on the name, but we shook hands anyway.

'What happened?' he said. 'Where've you been all this time?'

'I ran away.'

'You ran away. From what?'

I thought about this for a moment. 'Myself, I reckon.'

'Oh, yeah,' he said, nodding his head like he knew what I was talking about. 'The invisible enemy.'

I nodded my head like I knew what he was talking about, 'Yes, sir.'

Carpenter shuffled out of his office and locked the door, then pushed what was left of his reddish hair back over his head and wrapped a long college scarf around his neck. He'd grown a beard or maybe hadn't shaved for a while. His eyes were a pale grey. Some sandy bristles disguising his half-moon face.

'I heard about Randy Miller,' he said. 'The police came to see me. I can't say I knew him well, as he attended class less than you. But I'm very sorry all the same.'

'It went wrong,' I said. 'It was just a delivery job that went wrong.'

I took out the bone handled dagger and handed it to Carpenter who turned it around in his hands and held it to his ear like it was a seashell and might communicate something to him. He shook it gently then ran his hands over the beaded buckskin and pulled out the blade and gave a low soft whistle. Carpenter looked at me, and then back at the knife, and then back at me again like I was a liar or maybe a thief.

'Where'd you get this?' he said.

'It's what we were supposed to deliver,' I said. 'But it went wrong.'

'It's an original staghorn knife,' he said. 'See those stickmen carved into the bone? That signifies the number of kills made by a warrior. The ones with their heads on would have been taken prisoner and the ones without would have been scalped. It's hard to put financial value on an antiquity. Maybe you should take it to the Royal Museum. I can put you in touch if you like?'

'It belongs to someone,' I said. 'I'm going to make sure they get it back.'

'That sounds about right,' Mr. Carpenter said.

There was an awkward silence while we tried to work out what to do next. The burden being on me for showing up with nothing but a stolen artefact and a lame excuse for missing his class.

Eventually Carpenter spoke. 'What is it you want?'

'I don't want anything,' I said.

'Why'd you come here then?' Mr. Carpenter said.

'I'd like to thank you,' I said.

'What for?'

Well that stumped me. Maybe I was feeling sorry for myself and didn't have the nerve to admit it. I mumbled some apology for taking up his time and took back the knife and placed it inside my coat and started to walk away but Carpenter called out after me.

'Goodbye, John.'

I stopped and turned and said, 'My name's not John.'

'Really?' he said. 'Well, what is your name?'

'William Turner,' I said. 'My name is William Turner.'

*

There was a rumour the greasers had taken Romeo out to The Stockyards and put him through a meatgrinder and sold him for fish food down at the Islands. Somebody else said he'd made it back before escaping over the rooftops and running up to Nova Scotia where he worked his passage on a merchant cargo back to the old country.

The Duke had wanted a talisman to protect him from his enemies. When Quohog went missing they thought he'd cut a deal with Romeo. From that day forward The Duke became possessed of a strange sickness, and thinking himself immortal, was to be found directing traffic at an intersection near Queen and Mutual Streets. Most days, cars and people moved out of his way, but somebody forgot to tell the Toronto Transit Commission and The Duke got hit and dragged along by 50,000 lbs. of streetcar.

After that, the Children split or joined other gangs or maybe went back to their wives and children, sleeping in their beds and dreaming about the glory days of stomping on anyone who got in the way.

Back home things had settled down. Ray had grown his hair into a big wave and started wearing wide ties with colorful water birds on them. Flamingoes. Kingfishers, that sort of thing. He had a new girlfriend too. Big toothed Jenny with a big scarf wrapped around her big head. She came in for a tent trailer and Ray sold her a Roamer complete with shower stall and hot and cold running water. They were planning their vacation and Ray was busy plotting the route. There were booklets spread out over the coffee table.

Campcraft. Auto, Trailer, and *Pack Camping for The Whole Family.*

'Do you know,' he said, 'the size of the Canadian camping market?'

I did not know and made that clear by keeping quiet.

Ray nodded triumphantly. 'No,' he said. 'I didn't think as much.'

*

We never spoke about my mother, but when I looked in the mirror I saw her looking straight back. The same blood running through our veins. Maybe that's why Ray could never stand the sight of me. Sometimes I'd catch him staring and I knew he'd been thinking about her again. He was like a fish hooked on a barb: the corner of his lip fixed, his eyes shallow. You can't escape some feelings. You just have to lock them up and then let them out once in a while so you don't go mad.

Holding on to something that doesn't hold on to you will just make you sick in the end, so I destroyed my collection of postcards and left the last one unanswered.

Hey, Turner, it's hot over on the west coast and I got myself a new job working for a swish company downtown. Are you still with that girl with the boys' name? Ray told me about what happened. Don't let it get you down. There's always plenty of fish in the sea to fry. How quickly

the time goes. Hang on to every minute. Heartache comes to us all.
Happiness too.
Your loving Mother

As I lay on my bed, the sun played through the mosquito net, casting patterns across the wall. All the while the knife lay under my mattress like some curse. I decided to keep only what I could carry, and so wrapped the dagger up and carefully placed it in a bundle of clothes and donated them to the clothing giveaway program at The Native Centre downtown, leaving the parcel at the reception.

It would find its own way home from there.

*

I packed some paperbacks and tapes along with my clothes into a knapsack and checked through my documents. I'd been working all summer and had saved enough to go traveling and see some of the places I'd only read about. There was a map of the world on my wall. A one-way ticket to Paris in my wallet. I would find a new place to live. There would be trains and planes and I planned to thumb my way around Europe before returning home. But like Mr. Robert Frost said on that bestselling fridge magnet of his: Yet knowing how way leads on to way,

I doubted if I should ever come back.

MOUNT HOPE CEMETERY

The graveyard was deserted except for some blackbirds. One called out a song. Its breath visible in the cold air. I couldn't help but think it was a gift from Millboy.

A blackbird song for a daylight hour.

The birds perched on the headstones and in the crooked branches of the trees. Their fine feather coats beaded with rain as they watched us step through the long grass. Wild flowers broke through the weeds:

Electric blues. A flash of red. Some yellow.

Millboy wasn't hard to find. A pile of new earth and a simple wooden cross marked out his grave. I knelt down and felt the mud ooze through my socks as the bracken scratched at my ankles. I ran my finger across the simple brass plaque engraved with the name, Randolph Miller.

Frankie was crying now. Tears rolled down her cheeks and fell splashing onto the soil. 'I never heard anyone call him that,' she said. 'Not in his whole life. Not even Gramps.'

I took out the arrowhead and bent up the plaque and twisted it from the cross and threw it to one side and carved his name deep into the wood. Then I took his blue shirt and set a flame to it and watched the fibres burn and blacken before sailing away like ashes from a campfire.

The wind was blowing the leaves around. They spun like gold pennies and pushed up against the stone slabs or rushed down pathways looking for a resting place. The spring thaw had unlocked the dankness from the earth, filling the air with a dry muddy smell. Clouds sailed low across the sky. The birds were returning to the lakes and forests. Crossing Southern Ontario on their way back north.

Frankie stood up and brushed the dirt from her jeans. Her eyes red from crying. Her nails cracked and bitten down to the quick.

'I'll call every day,' she said. 'We'll write to one another and you can come and visit. You'll see. This is not the end.'

*

Kathy Lee was waiting in her Pinto at the Cemetery gates fixing her makeup. Every now and then she'd honk her horn like she had somewhere to go. I kicked the ashes from the shirt into the dirt and walked to the car and climbed into the back seat.

On the drive back to town we sat in silence and let the radio do the talking. The Carpenters singing something so sad I had to keep looking out of the window.

The sun cast a filter over the day as the images rushed past like cinematic frames: Pylons and streets signs; stores and restaurants. Past the banks, the flowers sellers, Sam the Record Man, the longest street and the top of the world.

They let me out at Union Station. The massive limestone columns. The endless trains. The fresh bite of the wind an excuse to wipe my eyes.

*

I recall him by his lazy eye and golden curls. A boy in a bright blue shirt and face burned brown by the sun. He waits for me in my dreams. Sometimes standing on a bridge. Sometimes running between the walkways downtown.

Too far out to reach. We were outlaws running from nobody.

No teacher knew our name.

BIOGRAPHY

Richard John Parfitt is a writer and musician. Born and currently residing in south Wales, he spent his teenage years living in Toronto. In the mid 1990s he was a founding member of rock group 60ft Dolls. As a writer he was shortlisted for the New Welsh Review Rheidol Prize, and has also had work published by "Planet: The Welsh Internationalist', 'The Conversation', 'The Portland Review' and 'Red Pepper Magazine'.

ACKNOWLEDGMENTS

I'd like to thank Third Man Books' Chief Editor Chet Weise for his support and excellent advice, and Benjamin Myers for his generosity of spirit. Also, thanks to Syd Bozeman and Amin Qutteineh at Third Man Books, and to Ruth Shade, Jon Gower, Gavin Cologne-Brookes and Emily Breeze.

NOTE ON SOME SOURCES

Atwood, M. [1996] Strange Things: The Malevolent North in Canadian Literature: 'Clarendon Lectures'. Oxford University Press

Bradburn, J. [2015] *Historicist: The egging of Yonge Street*. Torontoist

Flores, D. [2016] Coyote America: A Natural and Supernatural History: Basic Books. USA

Frost, R. [1961] *The Road Not Taken*. Holt, Rinehart & Winston: New York

Mourning Dove / Hu-mIs'-hu-ma [1933] Coyote Stories: Caxton [the Names]

Smallman, S. Grace. [2014] Dangerous Spirits: The Windigo in Myth and History: Heritage House